The Ghost of Hillcomb Hall

A Darkly Enchanted Romance

Joshua Ian

MOODY BOXFAN
BOOKS

Moody Boxfan Books

Contents

Chapter One

The Ghost of Hillcomb Hall

England, 1910

 Thunder shook the sky and the fat clouds, stained grey with threat, huddled closer together, crowding the heavens and looming with menace. When the rain fell, it was a torrent, a great wall of water on all sides of them, blocking sight and plunging them into near darkness.

Given the weather, Jonas Laurence congratulated himself on having the good sense to order an Austin with a roof covering. He sighed in frustration at the sudden gloom, closed the book he held, *Gifts for the Sheikh*, and placed it on the seat beside him. He hadn't the mind to concentrate on reading, or much else now, and he felt despondent. Usually, at this point in a prospective job, his head would be full of ideas of what he might do with the client's grounds. How he might transform something, implement the newest techniques he had learned, the sparks of imagination as he interpreted his latest preoccupations in art or fashion or architecture into flowers, shrubbery, borders, and features. His reputation as a landscape designer was buoyed in all the circles that talked of such things by his artistic flair. But there was no space at the moment in his mind for these ponderings.

Despite his efforts to ignore them, his thoughts were consumed by Pearson, and the mess he had made of that relationship. It was a particularly forlorn trip without Pearson, who often accompanied him posing as either a business partner or, most often, a valet or companion—which allowed for far more intimate moments during overnight stays. And having a valet in attendance when he visited aristocratic homes made him appear to be one of them, or at least, made him appear to be aspiring, and that was enough to satisfy their snobbery, in most cases. Of course, in London, they were discreet, but amongst their closest acquaintances and friends, there had been no illusions about their relationship. But one had to be especially careful outside the city. He glanced at the spot where he had placed the book and imagined Pearson sitting there. Any other trip, Pearson might have been reading himself or studying Jonas with a small smile teasing his lips. But no more. Pearson had declined Jonas's invitation to accompany him on this outing—a last attempt by Jonas at reconciliation—and informed Jonas he would be gone when he returned. Pearson had found his own set of apartments, though he didn't say where, and all Jonas had to look forward to now was an empty home and a cold hearth. It had made the weeks on the road even that much lonelier a task.

The car dipped and trembled, trying to maneuver the now malleable road. Jonas leaned forward to suggest they stop and wait out the storm when he saw Donaldson, the chauffeur, grab the steering column and yell out "whoa now!" as he might chastise a frightened horse. Jonas was tossed to the side as the car veered sharply and slammed to an abrupt stop.

He peeked out of the side of the automobile as Donaldson hopped out to right the vehicle. Jonas saw that the front left tire of the contraption had sunk into a hole in the road, which was filling with muddy water.

"Are we quite stuck?" he called out. "Should I help push or something?"

Inwardly, he shuddered at the thought. How would it look showing up at the grand home of his new clients soaked and covered in mud?

"Won't be a moment, sir," Donaldson bellowed back, cataracts of rain flowing off his cap. "We'll just give her some leverage shall we?"

The car rocked and Jonas fell back, sighing. The still falling rain felt threatening somehow. It had blackened the sky and erased any evidence of the wonderful early summer days they had been en-joying up to now. He had his partner at the architecture firm, Derrick, to blame for this particularly dreary sojourn. The inhabitants of Hillcomb Hall were somehow related to Derrick's wife. Jonas admittedly didn't listen very intently when Derrick had rattled off the seemingly endless list of relations. He seemed to have some sort of kinfolk, nobility or not, crammed into every corner of England. This household was headed by "Cousin Graham" and his wife, Vita, along with both of their mothers in residence. "Cousin Graham" was, of course, Graham Benson Grey, 5th Earl of Stanley, Viscount Nicolson. It all sounded lovely on a calling card, to be sure, but Jonas, frankly, could not care less about titles. So long as they had decent brandy on hand.

Derrick himself considered them an odd lot, apparently, and said any time spent with the trio in residence had given him a sort of queer feeling that he'd rather not revisit. His only suggestion to the actual design process Jonas would employ being that of a hedge maze in which, hopefully, one could get lost for days, "or forever, if their luck allowed."

The automobile bounced and Jonas was lifted from the seat.

"I say," he exclaimed, clutching at the doorframe. The car jerked again and then lurched forward.

"There we are, sir," Donaldson cried as he trotted around and swung into the driver's seat, drenched. "Right as rain."

Jonas settled back.

"Not, perhaps, the most welcome simile, Donaldson," he said with lifted brow.

The chauffeur chuckled as he set the beast of a machine on the road again.

Hillcomb Hall appeared to be a great medieval monstrosity of a thing, Jonas noted as the car got farther up the long and winding entry road cutting across the estate. It was, of course, only a century or two old but it had been constructed with the obvious intent of being commanding, in a historical fashion. The hall was surrounded by a deep forest of trees, ranging in type and size, and although they did not come very close to the house, they succeeded in helping to block out much of the sunlight. The driveway, crushed shell wet from the torrent, which made a discomforting slippery kind of noise under the car's tires, was cut through a copse of tightly packed ancient trunks. From the plans he had seen, Jonas knew that behind the house was a swath of open ground that led down to a lake. But from the front, the whole property appeared hemmed in, cloistered from the rest of the world, and deeply shadowed like some decrepit castle from a storybook. Though the rain had finally broken, and it was only yet mid-afternoon, the house sat in what resembled a cloud of night. A great blanket of fog clung close to the ground and the house almost seemed to float in his vision.

It was a forlorn and sad-making scene and re-minded Jonas of the depth of loneliness he had been feeling of late.

"Damn creepy," muttered Donaldson louder than he had intended. "Beg pardon, sir."

Jonas inclined his head and thought he couldn't have put it more succinctly if he tried. Damned creepy, indeed, and daunting besides. How in the world, he wondered, was he supposed to design a garden that gave any life or joy of light to such a dreary pile as this?

The home was built of a grey stone that had inter-spersed among it design elements made of a light yellow-brown plaster. Jonas imagined they had once been bright, and added some depth but over time, it had all faded into a cohesive façade of drabness. Even the wooden benches dotting its porticos and walkways had absorbed the weather and time to become dingy and colorless. On the whole, it was rather disquieting. The place itself was like a faded water-stained daguerreotype of an abandoned relic that had been hurled through time and left to de-compose.

At the front of the house, there was built a stone overhang that appeared newer than the rest. It was a sort of porch, through which a carriage could drive up to the entrance of the place, itself visible through three large arched portals. Given the area's apparent temperament for a deluge, Jonas thought this a very smart addition.

Through one of the arches he saw the door was open and, just in the frame, a man appeared like some haint emerging from the shadows. The door had not seemed to move, rather to materialize as an open mouth at the front of the house with the tall and thin creature hovering at its side. He wondered if the man might spread his arms and suddenly disappear back into the blackness as if by magic. He shook his head, chiding himself that he ought to get his imagination under control. Too many books read in the back seat during his travels, to be sure. He was at a lovely grand manor home at the end of a rainstorm, nothing more. Still, as the car came to a halt, he could not shake a sense of foreboding that had begun to unfold in him. He gazed at the dense forest all around and studied the trees, trying to convince himself that he had no reason for such emotion.

The man in the door was, of course, the butler. Up close he was less some weird apparition than a distinguished-looking middle-aged man. He was gaunt but stolid rather than dour, and Jonas felt relieved. He had been bracing himself, he realized, for some sort of gargoyle of a man straight out of *The Castle of Otranto*. The butler did however seem, much like the house itself, awfully faded. Despite his lack of great age, his hair was silver throughout, his skin was pale and ashen, and his eyes were more steely than blue.

As he stepped out of the car, Jonas was jolted by a sudden loud shriek from the woods, which sounded like a woman screaming in horror. He tried not to jump, but he couldn't help glance over his shoulder, rattled.

"You'll forgive the noise, sir," said the butler. "It's the foxes. The lord and her ladyship are not keen on hunts so they've quite overrun the forest."

Jonas now recognized the sound he had heard many a time before and felt silly for being frightened.

"Yes, of course," he said. "Just a bit slow in the mind from the monotony of travel, you know."

"Of course, sir. I am Mister Avery, sir, at your service."

Jonas nodded hello as Avery turned to Donaldson.

"Patrick, the Head Groom, is there waiting for you. To show you how to put away the car and so forth."

"Where's that, guvnor?"

"Just there," said Avery in an enervated tone of voice. He pointed straight ahead of the automobile. "At the end of the *porte-cochère*."

"The whaa—?" asked Donaldson as he turned his head. "Blimey, I didn't see him through the fog."

Jonas followed his gaze and saw standing at the end of the carriage port a youngish man in rough tweed trousers and shirttails. His intense, almost wild eyes and ruggedly handsome features made Jonas think of Heathcliff on the Moors, planted there with the fog swirling around his boots. He was not dressed for the cool air the storm had brought, but he seemed sturdy and hearty enough to withstand it. Jonas appreciated Donaldson's surprise as the man seemed to have appeared from thin air.

"Yes, it is rather thick, isn't it?" offered Jonas vaguely.

"It's the slope of the land, sir," replied Avery. "We are in a valley of sorts, and the weather does tend to accumulate. Shall we go in?"

Chapter Two

"Her ladyship should only be a moment," said Mr. Avery, as he took Jonas's hat and coat.

The main foyer was long, with a high ceiling and sparse decoration. Towards the end farthest from the main door were two matching tables on either side of the corridor, which sat beside entrances leading to other wings. A few large tapestries were hung on the walls down the length but did little to dwarf the space, and little more still to counter the chill of the air. Beyond that, a large imperial staircase that led to the upper levels dominated the space. Jonas's gaze followed the staircase up and stopped suddenly at the landing. He stifled a gasp.

On the landing was an enormous painting that appeared to be the height of two men or possibly more. It was a portrait of a man, an astonishingly handsome man. His dark hair was somewhat short and a few loose locks of it fell across his forehead and curled at the nape of his neck. He was swarthy with a prominent jawline and cheekbones, his lips full and his nose strong; features, in fact, that looked as if they had been carved by an artist rather than God-given. But what struck Jonas most were the eyes. They seemed alive, not mere pools of oil and pigment, but watching, seeing, knowing somehow. The eyes seemed to bore into him and it gave him a chill that ran to the back of his knees.

He jerked his head away and was rubbing his hands together to bring back some semblance of warmth when he heard footsteps and then the quiet tones of female voices. From an entryway beside one of the tables emerged a trio of ladies in descending height. He was struck by the tallest of them, whose features were broad and good-looking, and who moved with a regal elegance as if she commanded all in her sight. This must be the earl's mother. The way the three of them moved towards him, in unison, their steps matching, he was struck with a thought of the Graeae sisters of mythology. Except these were all handsome women, and not at all shriveled or bizarre, so likely it was the family name which had birthed the thought. Or perhaps, he thought, nervously pulling down his waistcoat to smooth its line, it was the way they studied him, all at once and intently. Like the three sisters who shared one eye between them, simultaneously seeing and knowing. He hoped they didn't also share a tooth for devouring.

He glanced back up at the painting far above and something in its expression suddenly seemed to taunt him, as if that were at all possible.

"Ah, Mister Laurence, I presume," said the tallest woman. "We have been looking forward to your arrival. Was the weather too awful then?"

"Only briefly," he answered.

"Good. Allow me to introduce us all. I am the Dowager Countess of Stanley, and this is my daughter-in-law, The Right Honourable Countess of Stanley, Victoria Adalyn Grey." She indicated the younger of the two women who accompanied her.

"Lady Stanley," said Jonas with a nod.

"And this is The Most Honourable The Dowager Viscountess Aldrange, Flora West Lytheton, Lady Stanley's mother."

Jonas gave another nod and a broad smile. "Lady Aldrange. It is so nice to meet you all."

"My mother-in-law can sound quite grand at times, a quality I much admire," added the young Lady Stanley with a nod to the Dowager Countess. "But, really, we're not much of ones for standing on ceremony, Mister Laurence. Please call me Vita, won't you? Everybody does. Mamma christened me Victoria, after her beloved queen, of course, but I think Vita much better suits me."

"Vita it is then, gladly. But only if you'll return the favor and call me Jonas. Whenever I hear Mister Laurence, I picture my father in his tweed jacket looking very smug."

Vita smiled. "Yes, I know exactly what you mean. Then we are agreed."

Jonas nodded.

"We've arranged tea in the drawing-room," said Lady Aldrange. "Won't you join us?"

"I'd be much delighted. I could quite use a very warm cup just now."

It was a lushly appointed drawing-room, with broad, tall windows, and Jonas was happy to see that some sunlight had managed to force its way through the storm clouds, and left the room far less dismal than the foyer. As soon as they were all settled, two maids appeared with trays of tea and cakes and sandwiches.

The ladies watched as he took his cup which Dowager Countess Stanley poured for him and selected a small sandwich. He sat back in his chair, stirred his tea, and placing the spoon to the side, he waited for the ladies to serve themselves. The dowager smiled at him, gave a small nod to the others and they poured their cups. They made a bit of small talk about the sandwiches and cakes and the weather and then the Dowager Countess regarded him with a studied look.

"Your surname, Mr. Laurence. You use the French spelling do you not? Is that a nod to your heritage?" she asked.

He took a sip, considering his response.

"My great grandfather was French, yes. And his son married a Turkish woman, in fact. So I suppose I am an amalgamation of sorts."

"Oh yes, I see it," said Lady Aldrange. "You have the look of the exotic."

"Do I indeed?"

Vita's eyes widened a bit.

"No offense intended, Mr. Laurence," the Dowager Countess added quickly.

"None taken, milady," he said. "No, I have no qualms about my parentage, nor how I achieved my station in life. But it is not often commented upon by people of a certain class, if you will." Vita smiled at this and lifted her teacup to her lips to hide it. "Then again, I suppose most aristocratic families only see what they want to see, despite what might be obvious." He paused. "No offense intended, of course."

The dowager countess laughed. "None taken at all, Mr. Laurence. I do hope we haven't offended you too greatly. You see, in fact, our interest is a joyous one, not one of judgment. I think you will find, when it comes to our equals in society, we are considered rather rebellious."

"Or odd, depending on whom is being asked," added Lady Aldrange. "In fact, I daresay you find it odd for the mother of a bride to be living in the family house so comfortably."

Jonas shook his head. "Of course not, milady."

Though in truth he had been surprised when Derrick had explained the inhabitants of the estate. Not for his own personal tastes, but for the fact that he knew it not typical of families such as these. Everyone had their place, no matter how inconvenient to reality.

"Once my husband passed, you see, and the estate went to Vita's brother, I had a new role. But I'm afraid my son's wife found me a rather cumbersome addition to her family. So when Vita was expecting,

I offered to come stay for a while to help care for the child. I haven't always trusted maids very much, you see. They have a way of knowing too much."

"Except for my own nanny, of course," added Vita, with a mischievous smile. "The two of them were always inseparable. And she seemed very good at keeping secrets."

"Now, Vita," chided Lady Aldrange as she continued. "I lived for a time in the large cottage on the estate here, in which Countess Stanley so graciously found room for me. A grand place it was, and we had such a nice little household, didn't we, Clarissa?"

"Yes, very nice, Flora," answered the Dowager Countess. She looked at Jonas. "But then one of those horrid storms came—this area is quite known for them—and ruined the roof."

"Quite," said Lady Aldrange. "So we both came here and took a set of rooms in the West Hall."

"And Lord Stanley doesn't object?" began Jonas with a smile. "Being always surrounded by women?"

The Dowager Countess chuckled.

"No, not my son. In truth, he's hardly here many months in a row at any rate. Business in the city keeps him so occupied. We have become quite the domestic trio."

"And Mamma is so good with little Rupert, so it is perfect," said Vita. "Of course eventually we will need to hire a tutor or governess to continue his education but for now, all is right." She set down her teacup. "Do you approve very much of boarding school Mr. Laurence?"

Jonas reached forward and retrieved a small slice of seed cake.

"Not very much, no," he confessed. "As it relates to growing the mind, that is. But then I think it is more a question of formation than education."

"'Formation'? How do you mean?" asked Vita.

"Only that, of course, a man can expand his mind quite broadly in a number of ways but school prepares him to move amongst society correctly and aptly." He took a bite of his cake, chewed it and swallowed. "But, then again, I was not born into society and did not benefit from such schooling. I taught myself mainly, so I am far less than an authority and perhaps more than a little biased."

"But that certainly makes the case then. You are quite intelligent and amiable Mr. Laurence," said Lady Aldrange. "Quite the picture of a gentleman."

"Indeed," agreed the Dowager Countess. "I have found most society gentlemen to be empty-headed and thick-necked, which makes for quite an internal imbalance."

The other ladies, and Jonas, chuckled at that.

"My son will like you, I think," continued the Dowager Countess. "He himself has never had much tolerance for the Etonian type."

She glanced at her daughter-in-law and they exchanged small, almost imperceptible nods. Jonas felt as if he had been sat for an exam and wondered if he was receiving a passing grade.

"Perhaps on your walk tomorrow, we can show you the kitchen garden as well," said Lady Aldrange. "We have had an early rash of raspberries, about which I am so excited. I am afraid I always exhaust poor Cook in my demand for raspberry fool. But, really, how is one to get through a summer without raspberry fool?"

And indeed Jonas was inclined to agree that he did not know.

"It sounds delightful, of course, but I preferred to go over the main grounds in the morning. I like to catch the landscape from all angles of daylight when I am planning."

"Yes, of course," said Vita. "I'll be happy to accompany you on a tour, though I am afraid I won't be much use in planning anything. Lord Stanley is in charge of the gardens, and we've conceded to him free rein. He has quite a passion for it, you see, and I have no head for horticulture, so I would be useless anyway. Better to let you two gentlemen settle it."

"Then might he like to accompany us on the tour as well?"

"Oh, I am sorry, I didn't mention. My husband isn't due back from the city until tomorrow afternoon. He had meant to be available today but something held him up. So you'll have to make do with me as tour guide; that is unless you would prefer to meditate on the grounds on your own."

"Not at all. I welcome a tour with you, and it will give me a chance to prepare my thoughts and questions for Lord Stanley."

"Splendid," said Vita.

"Now, we should let you rest before dinner," said the Dowager Countess. "You must be exhausted."

"This tea has gone a very good way to restoring my energy, but I wouldn't object to a rest."

"I'm afraid we've only had the electric in on the first level so far. Do not think us Luddites, I beg you, Mr. Laurence; we have been working hard to refresh the house in all modern ways. Which means taking out all these terrible gas fixtures and replacing them. You must forgive us for our lack of modernity, but we have installed fully functional WCs near every guest room and there is a bathroom at the end of each hallway."

"The joys of plumbing!" Lady Aldrange interjected with a little squeak and a clap of her hands. "You know, Mr. Laurence, I don't think you can really appreciate the magic of a hot running bath unless you are of my age."

"Mamma does love a good soak," added Vita.

The Dowager Countess looked at Lady Aldrange quite fondly. "She likes it when I read to her."

"While she is in the bath?" asked Jonas.

"Oh, yes," said the Dowager Countess, turning to him. "I have a special stool, you see, covered in oilskin should it get wet, that I put beside the tub."

Jonas raised his brows and fought back a smile.

"Do we shock you very much?" asked Lady Aldrange.

Her voice previously light and effervescent was now notably less so. Jonas found Lady Aldrange regarding him with an interrogating expression.

He cleared his throat.

"No, not at all, my lady. It sounds quite comfortable, in fact."

"Indeed," agreed the Dowager Countess with a nod.

The ladies rose and Jonas followed suit.

"And my doctor assures me," said Lady Aldrange, her tone exuberant again, "that is an absolute necessity for good nerves."

She reached up to adjust an earring and gave him a queer little look.

"But then," she continued, "One should not always listen to doctors, you know. I find they seem to have certain rigid ideas about what is natural and unnatural to the human body. Don't you find, Mister Laurence?"

What was she getting at? He glanced around, all the women looking at him behind shaded eyes.

"On the subject of nature, madam," he replied, "I think very many have much knowledge to gain."

"Quite well put," agreed Lady Aldrange.

Vita led him out of the drawing-room, and as he exited he turned to close the doors behind them. The Dowager Countess and Lady Aldrange were watching, and yet again he felt under inspection. As if on cue, they both smiled at him, in the exact same fashion and nodded. He turned back and extended his hand in front of him, gesturing to Vita to lead the way.

"I am glad you have come to visit, it will be nice to have some company about," said Vita. "Mamma will have someone new with whom to share all of her medical advice and holistic theories. She does so love them, and I am afraid she thinks we only humor her. Which, in a way, of course, is true."

"I shall be very happy to humor her as well. And I myself have an interest in herbals and their uses and applications, so we might teach one another."

"How delightful. And I think Graham—Lord Stanley—will very much like you. I anticipate you will be good friends."

She stopped as they came to the landing at the top of the stairwell. It was much darker here, almost as dark as nightfall. Vita reached out to one of the two small tables on the landing, both holding oil lamps, retrieved one, and reached into the drawer for matches to light the wick.

"It has been so overcast," she said, "the servants haven't thought to prepare the lamps so early. But not to worry, the fires have been lit in your room and all should be bright and cozy there."

She lit the wick and in the flare of the light, the giant painting above them sprung into sight. Jonas took a sharp intake of breath and a step back. The handsome face seemed to glare down at him in the half-light, the curve of his lips that had seemed like a smile from below now resembling a sneer. He swallowed and cleared his throat..

Vita followed his line of sight.

"It's quite the striking painting, isn't it?" she said. "I am so used to it now, I forget. It's Lord Stanley's grandfather, in fact, who helped turn Hillcomb into the grand manor it is today. Or, rather, was. He's awfully handsome, don't you think?"

Jonas cocked his head and blinked. When he looked at it again, the face above seemed far less threatening.

"Yes," he said. "I suppose he is rather good-looking."

"I think devilishly so. I often remark on it to Graham and he pretends to be jealous. Which is ridiculous, of course, and we laugh."

She turned to move up the final stairs and the full light left the painting. As Jonas proceeded, he glanced back and noticed that the eyes seemed to follow them nonetheless.

"I'm rather glad Graham was delayed. He would have arrived after dark tonight, otherwise, and I do worry about him on those slippery roads. The rain never seems to leave these days. Of course, I never seem to know when he comes and goes most of the time at any rate. We insist on keeping separate sleeping chambers, especially since the arrival of our son. It is thoroughly exhausting being a mother, I must say."

"Of course. And where is the young sir, now?"

"Off somewhere with one of the maids, I would imagine. I usually don't see him until he is brought down for supper. He doesn't eat with us, of course, he's far too young. But he presents himself to all the family and then it's off to change and to bed."

She paused and nodded towards a door that stood before them.

"Here is your room then," she said with a smile. "As my mother mentioned, all of the ladies of the house reside in the West Hall of the house. You're just next door to Graham, of course, so that will be convenient upon his return. Until then, I imagine it will prove to be awfully quiet over here, possibly downright boring." She gave him a little smile. "But should you need anything at all, do not hesitate to ring; our staff is, I think you'll find, quite willing. Otherwise, we'll see you for dinner. We do dress, but you needn't be too formal unless you prefer it."

"Very good. Many thanks, Lady—Vita," Jonas said with a small bow, and they parted.

Chapter Three

J onas entered the room and stopped just inside the door, caught by the sound of rustling. It seemed to him to be the sound of some creature, a mouse, or maybe something larger, and it seemed to be coming from within the walls. He took a step farther in and cocked his head to the side to listen.

He heard it again, and it seemed to be moving about. What could possibly be making such noise, he wondered. He went to the fireplace, where a large fire was burning with a healthy glow, and took down one of the already lit lamps, wandering over to the bed. Just then a clap of thunder sounded outside, making him jump. Suddenly, there was a soft thud from inside the walls and a sound like a low grunt.

He froze, listening. There was a small scratching sound and then a creaking noise as one of the panels of the wall began to shift.

"What the devil," Jonas muttered to himself, too unsure to move.

The panel of the wall swung a little farther open and he saw a small pale hand pushing against the green baize covering on the other side. He followed the hand to the arm and farther as it led to the sight of a short maid, in a slightly askew uniform, who held a bundle of linen balanced on one arm. Her expression looked halfway between embarrassed and irritated, and Jonas almost laughed from relief. He could have kissed her when he realized how silly he'd been reacting to nothing more than the noises of a maid in the servants' corridor. But, of course, he refrained.

Despite the load in her arms, the maid managed a small, if awkward, curtsy. This, dislodged a folded sheet, which Jonas dipped down to catch, returning it to the pile.

"Thank you, sir."

"Quite welcome.... Sorry, what's your name?"

"Sarah. Begging your pardon, sir. I was just come to finish making up the bed."

Jonas looked down and saw, indeed, that the mattress was bare. He smiled.

"We've just been that busy today and it's taken me a while to get the room situated," she said, moving towards the bed. "It hadn't been aired in a while so I wanted to make sure it was all proper for you. Only they keep the spare linens in the servants' hallway, don't they, and it's gone so gloomy, I couldn't half see with the door closed."

She had unfurled the linens and began to make up the four-poster.

"But of course, I couldn't have you coming in and having the place open and shut halfways. And then I went and dropped a load of sheets in there when I tripped. Covered in smut they got, they'll have to be boiled again. Old Tweedy'll have my head for that, she will. I think that's why she gave me this room anyway, on account of —" She halted in the midst of tucking in a folded corner. "Apologies, sir. I reckon I ought not to be talking to you like this."

Jonas was grateful for her prattle, it brought him back to earth and shook loose some of the weird atmosphere he'd felt since seeing that damned painting.

"No trouble at all. I was just stopping to see if my trunk had been brought up before I change for dinner. Please carry on."

She smiled and continued her folding and tucking.

"Your trunk's just over there, sir, by the wardrobe. Cecil, what'll be doing your valeting while you're here, has unpacked it."

"Please give him my thanks."

"If I must," Sarah said under her breath as she smoothed the bedding and stood back to appraise her handiwork.

"I take it you and this Cecil are not the best of friends then?" asked Jonas, amused by her response.

Sarah shrugged.

"He's all right, I reckon, as boys go," said Sarah. "But he does give us maids a hard time. Always bossing us about and playing little tricks on us for a laugh, to try to frighten us and that." She paused to fix her cap, a cross look on her face. "Of course, Old Tweedy says it's just how young men are, just the ways of them, when they don't have a *proper outlet*, she says, for their energy. She says they grow out of it. But, lord save us, he is nearly thirty if a day so I don't reckon I know when he'll grow more."

"Some men never seem to become anything but silly little boys, I'm afraid," offered Jonas in solace.

Sarah nodded with conviction. She surveyed the room.

"Would you like the fire refreshed, sir?" she asked.

"Yes, please, if it's no trouble."

She pursed her lips in such a way as to suggest she was biting her tongue but nodded anyway.

"You said Mrs. Tweedy—is that her name?"

Even kneeling before the fireplace, he could see the smile on her lips.

"Mrs. Tweedham, sir. She's the housekeeper."

"Yes, Mrs. Tweedham, naturally. You say she stuck you with this room—"

"Oh, I didn't say stuck, sir. Hardly not."

"Of course. She gave you this room for a reason?"

"Yes sir. On purpose like I think." She added some coals.

"What would that reason be?"

Sarah studied the fire for a few moments, using the small bellows to feed it higher.

"Well, she hasn't been happy with me lately. Says I talk too freely, she does."

"You mean, it was meant as a punishment then?"

Sarah stood, smacking her hands free of the coal dust.

"Oh, no, sir. Nothing like that at all. I didn't mean that exactly."

Jonas eyed her as she chewed her lip and glanced nervously around.

"Is anything wrong, Sarah?"

"Oh no, sir. Nothing wrong."

"Is there something wrong with the room then maybe?"

"It's not my place to say, sir, I'm sure. So long as you're comfortable."

"Is there some reason I wouldn't be?"

"I hope not, sir." Her gaze darted about before meeting his.

"Sarah, I do hate to press, but I feel there is something on your mind. Is there something I should know? I don't understand why you feel Mrs. Tweedham should give you this duty as penance if something wasn't right."

"No, sir. Only," she paused, unsure.

"Yes?" he encouraged.

"Only they say it's haunted, sir."

"Haunted?"

"Yes, sir. The room. They say there's a ghost what lives in this room. And Tweedy, she knows I listen to the stories and she knows they send me the right shivers, so she likes to poke, you see, sir."

"I do see."

"It's why we hardly ever use this room for guests, you see. But her ladyship insisted you have it on account of the view of the grounds—for your work with trees and that."

The corners of his mouth turned up. He looked forward to telling Derrick about his "work with trees and that."

"But surely you don't believe in ghosts, Sarah?"

"I would never have said so before, sir. Before I worked here that is. But I've seen them since."

"The ghost?"

"Not the one they say clings to this room, sir. But another. Ghost of a kitchen maid, she were, what died in a fire here a hundred years ago they say."

"And you've seen her?"

"Oh yes, sir. I wouldn't have believed myself if I hadn't, but I seen the mischief she made in the kitchen. Breaking plates, tossing bowls hither and yon, turning over the milk. She's a right little bitch she is. Oh!" She clapped her hand over her mouth. "So sorry, sir; begging your pardon, sir."

He let out a short bark of laughter and waved away her words. "No apologies, please. You needn't stand on ceremony with me. And besides, if what you say is true, she sounds like an annoying little bitch indeed."

"Oh, sir, you don't know the half," She scrunched up her face in earnest annoyance. "But they say the ghost who haunts this room is much more frightening. Ghoulish even. They say he's been known to—at night when the guests are sleeping—" her cheeks flared red and she faltered. "Well, it's not to be talked about really, the things they say."

Jonas was surprised at her acute embarrassment. He thought better to not further explore this topic. He didn't want the young woman to think he had crossed any line of propriety.

"Sarah, I do appreciate you being so forthright in warning me about the room. But I assure you I don't hold with ghosts or anything preternatural."

She gave him a confused look but nodded. "But, should I happen to encounter anything strange, I know exactly whom to consult."

She nodded. "Yes, sir. You need anything at all, just pull that bell."

"Much obliged, Sarah. Now if you don't mind I think I should like to rest a moment before dinner."

"Of course, sir."

As she pulled the panel of the hidden passage smoothly back into its slot in the wall and disappeared unseen down its corridors, Jonas settled himself at the writing desk near a window.

As comical as she might have been, Sarah's words rattled inside his brain for they touched on the strange vibrations he'd felt all around him since arriving. Possibly it was the environment itself, he thought with a glance towards the gradually darkening window. Although the estate was not so extremely isolated, it certainly felt cut off from the rest of the world, sequestered as it was in its shadowy, fog-blurred valley.

And then too, there was the physical house itself. One could almost feel the creep of time weighing down the large stones it was fashioned from. As if you could touch the stone and feel the pulse of all the souls who'd passed through in the last centuries. He could see why they made such an effort to modernize the place, to cut into this historical gloom. Things like that must prey on even the most solid of minds after a time.

On even a mind like his.

He retrieved his diary from his case and undid the lock. He recorded a few notes about the trip and his day, and then his mind came to settle again on Pearson. Jonas knew that he deserved a proper clout about the ears for his behavior there. He was filled with regret with how he had let that relationship crumble over the last few years. He knew that Pearson was a good man, and someone he could have made a life with. And yet Jonas had never been entirely settled, never fully accepting of that possibility. Something had always nagged at him from a corner of his mind, telling him that this was not the place he was meant to be, or the person he was meant to be with.

For so long, he had retained a habit of settling for the unattainable figure or for simple scamps whose only interest was a good time to be had. But he had grown weary of that. Pearson was the first person in a very long time who had made him think of abandoning these shallow ways. And, still, his time with Pearson, just like anything meaningful in his past, had come to a sad ending. On reflection, he knew somehow that he had always been running, not necessarily away from anything, but towards something. He was trying to run his way back to an idea of true love which he had abandoned years ago, before Pearson, before other frivolous distractions. Maybe it was that unattainable ideal which had slipped through his grasp; maybe his chance to ever reclaim something like it was long gone. Still, there was a need within him, a demand for the thrill that overwhelming love affair of the past had once given him, the unexplainable touch deep within that not even Pearson had brought. That none had brought since those days now lost to the past.

However unsure he felt of what love had in store for him, he did know that he had grown quite tired of the London scene. All the parties, the constant social shuffles, the men here and there whose names were barely learned before they disappeared from the narrative. Men who were either arrested or who escaped into a respectable marriage or who fled, frightened, back to their home villages. He needed something more now, something beyond the boredom of the ordinary and rote. London, in all its way, had grown lusterless, drained of blood. Perhaps that was why he craved his work in the countryside. Surrounded by the lush green, the ever-growing life, the vibrancy, he felt somehow at peace. Even if, still, he felt unattached, searching.

It had been a lonely set of weeks, this summer.

He recorded his thoughts until the light outside began to wane.

Screwing his pen shut, he tucked it against the spine of the diary and moved to the window to watch as the fog grew darker. The blanket of atmosphere stretched on and obscured much of the large expanse of landscape, but far down he saw the outlines of the lake. Its rain-dotted surface appeared ashen grey like the sky it reflected. He let his eyes wander over the lawns, which were stepped in levels as they came to meet the house. Each stepped area was surrounded by short stone parapets that were virtually invisible due to the ivy and shrubbery growing over them. The larger shrubs, once manicured he could tell, had grown out and over and took on the most distorted shapes. Plump on certain sides and reaching in claw-like outgrowths on others. The edges of the gardens had been overgrown with heather and gorse, and though the colors looked strong and healthy from the rains, they ran amok in such a way as to suggest impenetrable wildness. *What a strange and dilapidated place,* he thought as he leaned against the window frame and took in the scene.

Just then he saw a sudden movement in one corner of the furthermost garden. He moved forward, closer to the glass. Probably just a fox or a bird of some sort. And then, there it was again a little farther along the parapet, a great bellow of fabric, it seemed to Jonas, like a cape unfurling. Just as quickly the shape dropped below the wall, and he struggled to see in the dim light. He felt his eyes strained as he placed his hands on the cool panes of the window and urged himself to see what path the shape took. He could make out no more movement and he realized he was holding his breath.

A short, hard rap at the door made him jump.

Jonas shook his head at his nervousness and bade the caller enter.

A handsome ginger-haired man entered the room, and Jonas's mind left the shadowy dwellings it had taken at the window. Jonas was quite used to being lent a man to assist him when he visited many a country house. More often than not, the chap assigned was a new boy, green and nervous, a minor servant like a new footman in training, or even a hall boy. He knew that valeting for a guest like him was training, and typically he felt he was doing more to assist the young man than the other way around. But this man held none of those qualities. He was self-possessed and obviously proud, so much so that he gave off an air of something close to arrogance. He had the height and looks to make a first footman, and he wore his livery well. And he knew it. Jonas wondered that they would endow a specimen such as this fellow on a mere visiting designer, but then it was clear the family were eager to make a good impression on him. He had to admit that this went a good bit of the way.

"Sir," the man said with a nod. "I'm Cecil come to help you dress for dinner."

"Ah, yes, Cecil, thank you."

Cecil came forward and, stopping at the fireplace, stood staring at Jonas. Once again Jonas felt as if he were being appraised, and it unnerved him. It was quite one thing for his hosts to take stock of a visitor in their home. But for his valet to so plainly study him without demure was unusually bold. Cecil was a bold and beautiful man, Jonas thought, perhaps dangerously so.

"Sarah mentioned you would be valeting me," Jonas supplied as the young man offered nothing but stares.

"Oh, Sarah," Cecil said with a smirk. "I hope she didn't go on too much. She likes to chatter, our Sarah."

"She was a pleasant young woman."

"So no talk of ghosts then?"

"As a matter of fact, there was. She claimed that my room was haunted. It seemed to make her quite nervous."

Cecil chuckled. "She is a bit easy on believing, is Sarah. It may be her downfall one day, I wouldn't wager. But it's mostly just your garden variety superstitions and that."

"So you are not convinced that I shall run into any ghosts then?" asked Jonas.

"I don't believe in ghosts, sir. And even if there was the ghost they suggest what haunts this room, I think you yourself would be quite safe from any harm at his hands."

Jonas raised his brows.

"Would I? Why is that exactly?"

"Well, sir. From the stories they tell, this ghost seems to have a particular fondness for a certain type of gentleman. And I believe he would be quite fond of you, sir."

The tone in the valet's voice made Jonas's cheeks flush and he turned towards where his trunk had been deposited.

"Well, I suppose I should dress," said Jonas in his best aristocratic tones. "We wouldn't want to keep the ladies of the house waiting."

"At your service, sir."

He felt hands on his shoulders from behind and froze.

"Your jacket, sir," Cecil said quietly.

As he was being undressed and dressed again, Jonas was keenly aware of the young man's hands on him. They moved at a languid pace and the process was slow. He could feel that every inch of him was being measured. As Cecil's deft fingers buttoned his waistcoat, Jonas watched the fire steadily, avoiding any eye contact with the valet. That dangerous beauty he had instantly noted seemed to hover between them like a miasma.

"It's a pity you had to change, sir."

"Is it?" Jonas asked.

"Yes, the dark blue waistcoat you were just wearing brought out your eyes so much more than this white."

Jonas could think of no reply, so he gave none. He only cleared his throat and examined the mantelpiece.

Cecil moved his hands up and brushed the dinner jacket.

"Your work is in the gardens, is that right, sir?"

"It is, yes."

"Do you help chop down the trees and such, sir? "

"I'm sorry?" asked Jonas, taken aback.

"Only that you've got the arms and shoulders of a laborer."

Jonas gave him a look.

"I'm sorry, no insult intended," Cecil said with a playful smile. "In fact, quite the opposite. Most gentlemen that visit here aren't quite as sturdy as you are. Sir."

Jonas felt that familiar sensation on the surface of his skin. Cecil was daring for a servant, but Jonas supposed he didn't have much chance for diversion in so small a household. He must be used to taking fast hold of whatever opportunities arose. Had he been so easily read, Jonas wondered, as to inspire such directness? His mind retreated to thoughts of the great loneliness he had felt of late, to his missing Pearson. A fox with instincts as sharp as those Cecil appeared to have would be able to scent a need so strong. Still, it might offer a distraction to shake off the creepy tendrils of this place that had threatened to wrap around him since he left the comfort of the drawing-room.

"I fence, and a little boxing occasionally," he answered. "And I am an avid swimmer. I bathe regularly—in fact, only two weeks ago I was at a new facility in Birmingham on Moseley Road. Astonishing pool."

"Birmingham, that's where I'm from," Cecil said with a wide grin.

"Interesting town. And quite a change from the countryside. Why did you leave?"

Cecil broke his gaze. "Had to," he muttered. "No choice of my own."

The young man turned away, clearly not wanting to speak on the subject. Jonas laid a hand on his arm gingerly.

"I only meant," he said, "that it must have been an easier place for a young gentleman like yourself to find amusement."

Cecil caught his eyes, his look speaking his desire plainly.

"I make do, sir."

Jonas cocked his head and smiled. "Of that, I am sure, my boy. Most sure."

Cecil took a step so that their bodies were closer than before, even closer than when dressing. He slowly ran his fingers along the line of Jonas's starched collar, touching more skin than fabric, and brought them down to his throat, straightening his bowtie with a caressing touch.

"I think you'll find," said Cecil, his voice rough-sounding, "that I am very good at amusing myself, sir."

He stared at Jonas and tilted his head. Their lips might have touched quite easily, and there was a hitch in Jonas's breath. He could feel the heat of the valet's body beating against him, and he had to steel himself not to doing something quite untoward. His resolve was tested as Cecil pressed against him.

"Do you like amusing yourself, sir?" he asked.

Jonas blinked and cleared his throat. "Being on the road as much as my work requires, I, too, have sought out amusement where I could find it."

"It must get rather lonely, sir, skipping around these old piles, wagging your chin with old dowagers and half-deaf colonels."

"It has its concessions," said Jonas, holding Cecil's gaze.

"Does it?" Cecil asked.

He pressed against Jonas and they kissed. It was an electric kiss, and Jonas felt the warmth of it quickly spread through him. He hadn't realized how in need his body was. It had been a lonely set of weeks, indeed.

Cecil grabbed Jonas by the back of the neck, pulling him deep into the kiss, his tongue exploring, pushing its way into Jonas's mouth. And then he broke away. Leaning back, Cecil studied his face, lifting his fingers to trace the lines of Jonas's lips.

"I shall very much like touching you tonight," he said.

Jonas leaned in for another kiss, but Cecil held up his hand.

"Ah, ah, sir. No time for that now. You don't want to keep your hostesses waiting, or they may think you're ungrateful."

Jonas tried for his mouth again, but Cecil turned his head, smiling.

"You're a bit of a tease, aren't you?" said Jonas.

Cecil eyed him with a cheeky grin. "Just because I like to be in control doesn't make me a tease, sir.

"A bit of a scamp then."

"And if I am? Is there anything wrong with that?"

"No," Jonas admitted, grinning. "I was only just saying to myself how fond I am of scamps."

"Well, sir, maybe I will make you very fond then. After all, you posh blokes don't get to call the shots all the time."

"I should hope not. "

Cecil moved away and bounded around the bed towards the servants' passage.

"Then I'll see you tonight?" asked Jonas.

A smirk came across Cecil's lips. He lifted one shoulder in a shrug. "Possibly, sir. But then again, possibly not."

Jonas chuckled. "A scamp just as I suspected."

"But should I decide to visit, shall I bring anything for you when I come, sir, just in case? Anything special that might give me good reason to come late in the evening?"

Jonas considered for a brief moment. "A cup of tea?"

Cecil gave a bemused grin. "Tea? Brilliant, sir."

"Is it? I always have a cup of tea before I retire in the evening, to help me relax."

"We must make sure you are relaxed then mustn't we, Mister Laurence."

"Assuming," added Jonas, "that it isn't too late for tea."

"I shouldn't think you'll be kept too long," Cecil said. "Her ladyship never likes to stay late. Has to look in on her prized stallion, doesn't she."

"I'm sorry?"

Cecil bit his bottom lip and gave him a look as he backed his way to the service panel.

"I shall look forward to seeing the evening unfold, sir," he heard Cecil call softly as the panel clicked shut.

Chapter Four

M oving down the darkened hallway, Jonas wished he had asked Cecil where the dining room was as he knew not and the chill had already settled back on him only a few steps away from his room. As he gained the stairwell, he paused on the landing and lifted his lamp, once again regarding the overbearing visage of Grandfather Stanley. The eyes seemed even more devilish than before and chilled Jonas to the marrow. Was it his imagination or did the painting's smile now seem to be an expression of disdain?

Once again he felt as if the painting somehow saw into him as a real person might; once again it seemed to taunt him.

"Bah," he said aloud and dismissed the painting with a wave.

"Are you quite all right, Mister Laurence?"

He turned, startled, to find Vita's mother waiting for him at the bottom of the stairs.

"Oh, Lady Aldrange," he said. "I didn't see you there."

She was giving him that same gimlet-eyed look from the drawing-room. For all her supposed frivolity, he could tell that she possessed quite a bit of insight.

"Yes," she said, her voice light, "Clarissa thought I ought to make sure you knew the way to the dining room."

"Quite," he said as he descended. "Thank you."

"It's quite a picture, isn't it?" she said when he reached the floor.

"Yes, indeed."

"Are you very much attracted to it?" she asked.

"There is something oddly compelling I must admit," said Jonas. "For some reason, I feel as if I ought to know the man in the picture, but, of course, that's ridiculous."

"Maybe not so ridiculous, Mister Laurence," Lady Aldrange said with a smile.

He glanced back up at it and shook his head.

"I apologize," he said. "I think I am over-tired from my trip. A good dinner will serve me well."

Dinner did, in fact, serve him quite well. After being introduced to the young Master Christopher, a bright boy of about three years of age, who looked just like his pretty mother, only differing in coloring, a maid took him to his room. The wine was free-flowing and the food was delicious, one of the best meals he'd had of late. The dining room, like the drawing-room, had most evidently been recently redecorated; it was open and fresh-feeling, and the electric lights gave it a warm and welcoming glow. It was as if coming down the stairwell, he had entered into a different household entirely. The conversation was convivial and peppered with laughter.

"Might I ask," ventured the Dowager Countess as they ate, "how you got your start in landscape design?"

"I was articled to Messrs. Lansear and Sons in London," said Jonas. "That is, in fact, where I became fast friends with your cousin Derrick. While there I also met Lady Gertrude and she and I got on tremendously well. I had always had a personal interest in gardens and all that, but never really thought of it as someplace I could devote my creative interest. She opened my eyes to the possibility through her work, and she took me under her wing. I was apprenticed to her, if you will, for a few years and then Derrick and I decided to start our own firm with a fellow architect he was associated with."

"Lady Gertrude, how marvelous," said the Dowager Countess.

"Do you know her?"

"I know much of her, of course, but I do not know her very closely on a personal level, unfortunately. However, I have had the good fortune of working with her at a number of meetings."

"'Meetings'?"

The Dowager Countess exchanged a glance with Lady Aldrange, who inclined her head.

"For the purposes of advancing suffrage. You see, I'm a suffragette. We believe in the vote for women. I assume you're familiar?"

"Oh, I am quite familiar, indeed," he said with a smile.

She gave him an arch look. "Do you sneer, sir?"

"Not at all, you misunderstand me, your ladyship. You see, I am a bit of a suffragist myself."

Lady Aldrange seemed surprised.

"You?" she asked.

"Quite. I first learned of the movement through Lady Gertrude, actually, and I wholeheartedly support it. I am afraid I can't be too vocally open about it as so many think it's bad business for a man to be mixed up with such affairs. So the partners insist I keep my leanings under the hat. As I am used to keeping quite a bit under my hat, I manage. But I am a member of the Men's League for Women's Suffrage and I have helped to facilitate some meetings for the women's leagues—acquiring disused buildings for workrooms and that sort of thing."

"How extraordinary," exclaimed Lady Aldrange. "I have never heard of a male suffragette."

"There are a few of us, though not many, unfortunately."

"You will make an extraordinary match for my son," said the Dowager Countess.

"'Match'?" asked Jonas. He reached for his glass but noticed the smallest of silent exchanges between Vita and her mother-in-law.

"What I mean is, he is the only other man I have met with such forward-thinking views as yourself.

He is not part of any league as far as that goes, but he is quite the modern thinker. He despises what he calls the Etonian Type—those men he grew up with at school, and their staid ways."

Jonas nodded. "Then I think we shall get along splendidly indeed."

"Oh, I very much hope so," said Vita. He caught her gaze and noticed a strange intensity there. "He could very much use a *proper* friend."

Friend? wondered Jonas. But he was merely an employee, a consultant, really.

Just then a volley of screams from outside broke through their conversation. Startled, Vita dropped her fork onto her plate.

"Those damnable foxes," cried Lady Aldrange. She turned to her daughter. "I know you and Graham do not approve of blood sports, dear. But really something must be done."

"Mamma, you know we object to hunts. Graham would never want all those boorish neighbors of ours roaming the land with their guns. It's unconscionable, really."

"I have always thought," said Lady Aldrange, "that foxes make a very conscionable fine ladies scarf or trim for a hat."

"Oh, Mamma, really. Don't be horrid."

"She finds me quite brazen at times, Mister Laurence," said Lady Aldrange, her eyes bright. "It is always thrilling for a mother when she can still manage to astonish her daughter."

Jonas nodded and smiled.

"Quite," he said.

They all adjourned to a second drawing-room, this one even more spacious than the tea room, after dining. Seeing as there were so few of them, and him the only gentleman, no one saw the need to separate as might customarily be done in other houses. Both he and Vita took brandy and the elder ladies a sherry, or three. They discussed music and books, shared interests that all four of them were passionate about. Vita herself was particularly interested in hearing about any theatre he had partaken of in the city and lamented that they did not get out more often to enjoy the stage. Jonas suspected she might harbor a yen for an audience herself as she soon moved onto playing for them on the piano. She played well and had a strong clear voice, though her choice of song, Jonas thought, was a bit odd. A ballad, from America she told them, of a woman whose husband had bludgeoned her to death on the evening before their wedding and thrown her body into the river. Her performance was so engaging that he got lost in the story, and by the time the final notes faded, he felt a shadow move again across his spirit. Nothing another drink couldn't help, to be sure.

"Would you mind pouring me another sherry?" asked the Dowager Countess as he moved to the drinks cabinet.

"Not at all."

The drinks cabinet was quite near to a set of large French doors, which took up most of the wall on this side of the room and looked out onto the grounds. As he poured the glasses he studied a piece of the estate he had not yet seen. Not too far off the land here took a sudden slope that became a hill leading to a copse of birch trees framing the line of the forest. Their slim trunks were contoured by the moonlight, and through them, he thought he could just discern the outlines of a building of some sort.

He squinted trying to make its full shape but could not in the darkness. Lifting the sherry decanter to pour a drink, he was caught by sudden movement outside. He saw nothing. His imagination again, he decided, as he reached to replace the crystal stopper. And then, suddenly, a whirl of black, like the figure of a man in motion cut across the white surface of the hidden building and then from inside swelled a glow of light, as if from a lantern. The stopper missed the decanter and fell with a thud.

"Everything all right?" asked Lady Aldrange.

"Apologies," Jonas answered. "Clumsy fingers."

When he glanced back outside, the light was gone. He could only just make out the trees now, and the moonlight seemed to have hidden itself behind the clouds, the form of the building now obscured.

"Do you plan to drink my sherry yourself?" The Dowager Countess asked with a laugh. "I'm not entirely sure it mixes well with brandy."

"I apologize, your ladyship," he said, bringing her the sherry. He took a sip of his own drink. "I was just caught off guard by what appeared to be a building in the forest there, just beyond the small cluster of birch trees."

"Oh, that's just the folly," said the Dowager Countess. "My husband's grandfather had it constructed for some reason I know not. Of course, the servants thought he built it for romantic trysts in the night but who can say. No one uses it anymore at all. In fact, it's crumbling. Many's the time I've wanted to have it torn down."

"So no one goes there anymore at all?"

"I can't see why they should," answered the lady and then laughed.

"Why do you laugh?" he said, smiling.

"Oh, it just reminds me of the story of that maid," she said. "Constance I think her name was. You see, the servants have always claimed that the folly is haunted. The lover of one of the past earls was killed there or took their own life, or who knows what. You know how servants will gossip. But, in actual fact, they think half the estate is haunted, of course. So why not the folly too? It's all quite ridiculous really."

"And this maid, Constance?"

"So the story goes, she apparently swore to have seen something that shocked her so badly she couldn't speak for days. She refused to ever pass the folly again, my husband said," Lady Stanley shook her head, laughing again. "She was a kitchen maid, and the laying houses were on the other side of the trees there. But she refused to go, or took long circuitous routes instead. She became rather useless if it involved going outside of the kitchen, in fact. But eventually she moved on and found another house to work in."

"One with fewer ghosts perhaps," added Vita, with a wink.

"What could she have seen that shocked her so much?" Jonas asked.

"Who can say, my dear boy?" said the Dowager Countess. "Some of the staff, especially those from small villages, are so easily shocked. Still mired in ancient superstitions, you know. As well, this Constance was the daughter of a vicar, and you know how they can be—the slightest thing shocked her beyond repair. Lord Stanley—my husband—told me he once recalled hearing her gasp when his father kissed his mother's hand outside the church of a Sunday. She really was a silly little thing. And then, of course, there was the rumor that she didn't actually find employment elsewhere—that, in fact, she was murdered. Or drowned in the lake or something."

"Really?" Vita said, her voice full of surprise. "Graham never told me that."

"I expect he thought it was as ridiculous as we all did," said the dowager. "There was, naturally, no evidence to suggest murder. The only talk my husband ever heard of it was through servants, and, as I've said, they have their reasons to believe there is a ghost in every empty room."

Jonas eyed the line of trees. Ridiculous maybe, he thought, but he was starting to have his suspicions.

"Flora, come and help me to bed," said the Dowager Countess. "It's well beyond the hour to tell stories, and I believe I have overindulged in sherry."

The older ladies said their goodnights as Jonas glanced over the few books on a nearby shelf mainly peopled with ornaments.

"Are you fond of reading?" asked Vita.

"Oh, yes, quite fond. A good book goes a long way when you travel as much as I do. It helps me retain my sanity—at least, I hope so."

"The family library is just in the room next door. Please feel free to borrow anything that might be of interest. I'm afraid those few there were chosen more for their colorful spines and binding than for content."

"Thank you, then," said Jonas. "I just might take you up on that. Shall I pour you another brandy?"

"I've had my fill, I'm afraid. I might as well retire too if it's not too rude. I am not one for late nights."

"Not rude at all; of course not. I appreciate you're keeping me company this evening."

"I'm sure Graham would have done a better job, but I am glad you have enjoyed yourself thus far. Please enjoy the fire, the drinks, and the books for as long as you wish, with my compliments. There is no one about to disturb so don't mind the hour. I'll have the maid leave a lit lamp on the landing for you."

"Thank you, your ladyship. It has been a lovely evening."

"You're quite welcome, *Jonas*," she said with a smile.

"Yes, of course," he said, smiling back.

He sat by the fire for a bit longer nursing his drink, and then felt the fatigue of the day settle upon him. Though he doubted he would need a book to sleep—especially if the promised diversion of Cecil proved to be true—Jonas decided to pop into the library to have a look just in case. Libraries were always a favorite room of his and he relished getting to see the grand ones found in homes like these.

This library was certainly far from disappointing—in fact, it was one of the most magnificent he had encountered. The perimeter was full of shelving, in rich, dark oak, running from floor to ceiling, with multiple ladders on casters and plump stuffed chairs scattered throughout. He reached for the light switch but paused. On the opposite side of the room was a large window, the drapery drawn open, and from it moonlight cascaded down over a large swathe of the shelves, picking out the gold leaf of the bindings and making the inscribed titles practically dance in the darkness. He thought it a magical sight and gazed for a second before moving towards the window.

His eyes were moving down the lines of books as he stepped in front of the window. He pulled down a title and stepped back, looking at it in the light of the moon. Not anything he had heard of but he flipped through the first few pages. Glancing up, he noticed that this window faced the same area of the estate that he had studied from the drinks cabinet. The moonlight seemed fuller now, and he peered towards the line of trees now familiar to him. He could just notice the outline of the roof of the folly highlighted against the darkness of the forest. And then, just like before, a light came from within it. He blinked, leaning forward to make sure he was not imagining it. But there was indeed some sort of lamp or lantern lit within the folly. That could be the only explanation for how the source seemed to move around inside the small building, with its arches and columns. He was sure one could see straight through the folly in daylight but the cloak of night hid portions of it. Against one visible bit of wall, shadows seemed to move in the light. He could not quite make them out at this distance, but as they overlapped and pressed together, it struck him that there must be more than one person—or indeed, creature inside. The light stopped moving yet the shadows continued. He wished he could open the window so as to hear what might be heard, though from so far away, it was likely nothing.

He decided to test an idea, and reaching behind him, he flipped on a nearby desk lamp. The electric light burst into the darkness and lit the entire corner. He turned and noted that the lamp light within the folly was immediately extinguished. Standing in the frame, he waited, studying, to see if the light might return. Acutely aware that he was now visible in the lamp's glow, he became self-conscious. He returned the book he was holding to the shelf and clicked off the desk lamp. Slipping to the side, he moved as if he were leaving, but instead pressed himself against the wall, and peeped through the drapery around the frame of the window. After a few moments, the light flared inside the folly again, and the moving shadows returned. There was a great bit of movement if the shadows could be trusted, and then the light went out. He stood there moments longer waiting to see if it came back on before chiding himself for acting like a spy or a Peeping Tom. If some sort of clandestine activity was being conducted on the estate, surely it was no business of his. He gave up on finding any reading material and headed for the stairwell.

On the landing, he retrieved the one lit lamp and glanced up at the giant painting. The former Lord Stanley seemed to look at him with lifted brows.

"I'm sure you've done some spying in your day as well," he said under his breath.

Just then he thought he heard some footsteps coming from the East Hall, in the direction of his room. He quickly ascended the next few stairs and held up his lamp. Nothing could be seen or heard, so he made his way to the bedroom.

Inside his room, the fire was going at a very comfortable roar, but he was alone. He glanced about, wondering if Cecil had yet to arrive, but he saw his nightshirt laid out on the mattress. A small twinge of regret fluttered within. He had met Cecil only hours ago, and of course, had no real attachment to the man, but he had to admit could do with a bit of company. This house, for all the pleasantness of its inhabitants, had left him feeling rather cold and alone.

As he changed into his nightshirt, he noticed the cup on his bedside table. He smiled. Even though their rendezvous had fallen through, the man had brought him the promised cup of tea. Between his exhaustion and the alcohol, he doubted he needed any inducement to sleep, but he thought he would take a bit anyway. He sat on the bed and brought the cup to his lips, sipping the lukewarm liquid. He drew back from it, grimacing. The bitterness was beyond measure, and it tasted like no tea he had ever had. It was a kind gesture, he thought as he placed the cup back on the small table, but he would have to pass on anymore.

Jonas felt he ought to be awake, but he couldn't be sure. There was some noise, like a low humming that made him open his eyes. He felt as if he were underwater. His head was swimming, and it ached. Not as much like a pain but like a heavy weight pulled against it, trying to drag him into unconsciousness. But he wanted to awaken. He tried to sit up but his body would not cooperate. His limbs felt as if they were made of stone. He blinked, trying to focus, but all around was pitch-black. Somewhere in the distance, he heard a sound like thunder, like the beat of rain on a rooftop. And closer still, the humming. He was still in the bed at this place, this Hillcomb Hall, he could sense that. He turned his head, with what seemed a huge effort towards where the windows ought to be. But they were dark, part of the blackness, the drapes closed, as if they had never been there, in fact. Only a wall of black. The fire, too, seemed to have burned down or been extinguished as it cast no light.

He closed his eyes and the blackness was the same. The humming came back, and then a touch, fingertips grazing down his legs. He opened his eyes but could see nothing. The humming stopped. The fingertips turned to hands and the hands moved up, caressing his thighs. Again he tried to sit up but was unable. He tried to move but his limbs were like logs beneath him. It was as if he were strapped to the bed, weighed down by some invisible, mystical force that had total control over him. Still yet he felt the hands, squeezing the hard curve of his thighs and moving in between, moving up, up. Up until a hand cradled him, his most delicate part in its warm palm. Another hand came and began to stroke him through the fabric of his nightshirt. *No*, he tried to call out, but his voice was nothing but a gasp, no form, no words. He tried to lift his head but it lolled back. He let his face fall against the pillow; felt its cool material against his cheek.

The hands moved back down and slid under his nightshirt, pushing it up the length of his body. Again he tried to speak, but he heard a sound like a soft hiss. A voice he did not recognize shushing his protests. *No*, it said, in a ghostly whisper. Its hands, moving like a phantom pushed the material up until his whole body from the chest down was exposed. His arms beside him would not allow him to bend his elbows to try to feel the presence manipulating him. *No touching*, the hissing whisper warned. And then he felt lips, kisses on his skin. Up and down his torso, around his belly button, and then back up. What felt like a tongue brushed against one nipple and then another, sucking lightly, teasing him. He turned his head again, lifting his chin and tried to moan. But he wasn't sure if anything escaped his throat but a rough sigh. The kissing lips moved down, down below his navel, the tongue licked him where he had begun to grow, powerless to stop his body's response. The mouth kissed, licked, sucked; the hands moved over his thighs, over his stomach, stroked his shaft.

The touches felt like electricity, as if every part of him were static energy, as if they could melt through him; they shimmered against him like stormy winds, rumbled against his skin like thunder. The mouth enveloped him, drained him. And then, like a flash of lightning, his head thrown back, he was spent. He felt the ragged sighs tear from his throat and he clenched his eyes shut. He could fight it no longer and fell back into the blackness of sleep.

Chapter Five

Jonas blinked awake and tried to focus. He felt groggy and shook his head to try to clear the fog. He pulled the bedclothes closer, almost to cover his face, in order to fight against the chill. It was positively arctic in the room. He shivered and let out a little moan of discomfort.

"I should have the fires going in just a tick, sir."

Hearing Sarah's voice, he sat up in bed.

"Oh, Sarah, I didn't realize you were here."

"I'm meant to be invisible, sir, so that is good to know. Apologies for how cold it is in here. Her ladyship said not to disturb at all until you were ready, so I didn't come in early as I might normally have done. But I didn't want to leave it too long."

"Is it as late as all that?"

"Not terribly, sir. But you have slept through breakfast. Her ladyship said it was probably on account of all your traveling that you would be exhausted. She said we can gladly bring up a tray if you like."

"Is lunch soon?"

"Not for a couple of hours yet."

"Then I think I shall be all right with some coffee if you have it. And a spot of toast. "

"Of course, sir."

Sarah had gotten the fire going well and she stood, removing the detachable sleeves meant to keep the soot from her uniform.

"As well, Cecil says to send his apologies," she said.

Jonas blinked and shook his head again. "His apologies?"

"Yes, sir," she said, gathering up her items. "He was meant to attend you last night but the butler called him to a task that needed tending immediately. So he wasn't able to be of service and he asked me to lay out your clothes. And what with her ladyship saying to leave you be, he weren't here this morning either to dress you."

"It's quite all right. I am quite independent, really," he replied. "So you were in my room last night Sarah?"

"Yes, sir."

"Then you left me the tea? I wondered what type it was, it was unusual to me."

Sarah frowned. "The tea, sir?"

"Yes, the tea...." He turned to point at the bedside table but it was empty. He looked around, trying to spy the cup. "Where has the cup gone? Did you remove it?"

"The cup, sir? I'm sure I wouldn't have."

Jonas was perplexed. "There was a cup of tea by my bed last night when I returned. Rather bitter-tasting stuff, I must say. And I wondered if it were really tea at all."

"I'm not sure of any tea, sir." Sarah glanced around the room as well, as if she might help solve the mystery. "I didn't bring any last night, and there was no cup when I came in to light the fires just now. And you were very much asleep then, so I don't think you would have moved it."

"I was snoring then?"

"Well, I wouldn't say, sir."

"But you saw no cup?"

Sarah was very earnestly involved by now. "No, sir, I did not, come to think. The only thing I could see was the glass there by the water pitcher."

Jonas was beginning to feel a bit silly. "I'll be damned. How odd. I could have sworn.... Anyway, thank you, Sarah. It is not important, really."

She nodded and headed towards the service panel.

"Shall I fetch Cecil to dress you then, sir?"

"No, no, thank you, I'm quite capable. Just the coffee and toast would be splendid."

When Sarah had left, he got out of bed, groaning as he stood and clutching his head. Too much brandy in the drawing-room; that must have been it. The excuse for his wild fantasies at night: too much brandy and too much imagination altogether at play. But had he dreamt up a cup of tea? It seemed a strange thing to create. Yes, he was used to taking tea before bed, but why would that linger in his mind and the bitter taste as well. What had he drunk? It made no sense, but yet another odd thing about this house that confused him.

Just like the bizarre dream he had had, which felt so real. But how could it have been? He had no use of his body or his voice, what sort of thing could have done that? If he did not know better, he would have sworn he had somehow been possessed—as if some spirit or haunting had taken control of his body. Where had these thoughts come from? He had never been one to revel in the gruesome imaginings of haints and spooks before. This house had done something to warp his mind, he was sure of it. Maybe the place really was inhabited by some malign spirit that set up visitors to make them feel as if they were losing their senses.

Or maybe, Jonas, he told himself, *it was one night of bad sleep in an unfamiliar place during a rainstorm.* He nodded and rubbed his hands together as he sat at the small writing desk to record his thoughts in his diary. It would be amusing, he thought, to look back on that odd nightmare when he was again in the comforts of his London home. And coffee would help him clear his mind, ever the anchor for a day of work. He hoped, in fact, Sarah might bring a small pot. He wanted to be alert as he toured the grounds, there was a good many things he wished to examine.

As he came downstairs, he encountered the Dowager Countess and Lady Aldrange in the foyer.

"Ah, Mister Laurence, I trust you slept well?" asked Lady Aldrange.

"Well enough, I should imagine."

"Yes, it is always a challenge the first night on a new bed, isn't it? One never can adjust properly," said Lady Aldrange cheerfully.

"I'm afraid you've missed breakfast," said the Dowager Countess. "But you can gladly ring for something if you like."

"Quite all right. I've been provided with coffee and toast."

"Good," said the Dowager Countess. "We have decided to take a walk into the village. We don't like to take the horses out after such a storm, but your man Donaldson took the automobile out this morning—he tells me it's good for the engine—and assures us that the roads aren't too tragic after yesterday's storm. We may stop over for lunch, of course."

"Is Donaldson about?"

"Oh, yes, he's just out giving the machine a polish now."

"Then I must insist you allow him to give you a ride. Unless you prefer the walk, of course."

"We do enjoy walking—"

"Oh, Clarissa, I would enjoy a ride in an automobile!" interjected Lady Aldrange. "Graham has one, of course, but he has it with him in the city so often that we hardly get a chance to ride in it. Vita has talked of getting one for the house ever since little Christopher was born, but between one thing and another, we still make use of our carriages."

"Then you must, I entreat you. You said the weather here is very unpredictable and Donaldson loves any excuse to be on the road."

"Well, if you're sure you don't mind," said the Dowager Countess, "that might be much more comfortable."

"Oh, indeed!" cried Lady Aldrange. "And speaking of horses, Mr. Laurence, Vita should be back shortly. She's gone for her morning ride, she always does after breakfast. She has developed such a fondness for horses since moving to Hillcomb."

"I look forward to her return."

"The sketches!" proclaimed Lady Aldrange. "I had almost forgotten about them. You mentioned that you might do some sketching after your tour with Vita today. So I found a series of watercolors I did with Graham some many months back. We based them on current areas of the garden, and he gave me instruction on how he envisioned changes which I tried to translate onto the paper. I thought they might be useful for reference?"

"They would be a great help."

"Good, Vita will show them to you."

Jonas helped them into the car, and although Donaldson had just finished polishing, he did not at all seem put-out at the prospect of more muddy roads. With a wave Jonas saw them head into the village.

As if on cue, from the east side of the house Donaldson saw Vita coming up the sloping lawn. She wore a fine riding habit, side saddle style, of green and black piecing. Her cheeks were rosy and her hair slightly mussed, but otherwise, she seemed quite re-laxed and the picture of health. It was a comforting sight to Jonas, after his evening of weird ideas and disconcerting dreams.

"Good morning, Vita. I've just seen your mothers off to the village."

"Splendid," she said. "Shall we begin our tour now?"

"Unless you would prefer to change?"

"Not at all, this is perfect for tromping round the grounds. Come, let's start on the east side since we're here."

She took him down the sloping lawn, which was more like a hill really and they chatted about all of the different types of trees that had been plant-ed throughout the years. The birch trees, which he had noticed the night before, seemed rather anemic against the lush and full greenery of the oaks and elms behind them, but in a way, they lent a charm to the setup.

"There's the folly I noticed," said Jonas, pointing. In the daylight, he noticed how sturdy it appeared. It was in a rather dated faux-Corinthian style but not a particular eyesore nor as dilapidated as the Dowager Countess's word had led him to believe.

"Do you still make much use of it?" he asked.

"Use of it?" replied Vita, sweeping back some ten-drils of hair from her face. "For what exactly?"

"Oh, garden parties, fêtes, county fairs, that sort of thing."

"Oh, yes, I see." She shrugged. "It has never oc-curred to me, really. As squires of the land, and all that, we haven't done much in the way of enter-taining since I came to Hillcomb. But it's an idea. Despite what my mother-in-law says, I don't see any need to demolish the thing. I'm sure it can be handy."

"Yes, quite handy, I'm sure," said Jonas. And if his thoughts strayed to the secretive comings and go-ings he must have borne witness to the night before, he did not let his tone indicate it.

As they turned a corner of the house, they were greeted by a great outcropping of a structure which surprised him. He stopped and examined it.

"That's the old chapel there," offered Vita.

"I haven't seen anything like that in ages," said Jonas.

Much like the great house had been constructed in the style of a building from far earlier than its actual construction, so, too, had the chapel been made to look archaic. It suggested some medieval gathering place, like the earliest church of a peasant village. But, unlike the house it seemed so clumsily attached to, the facade did not hold up. Despite its attempt at crude art, it felt overly intentional. Even the ivy which climbed the sides, threatening to overtake the whole structure, seemed to have been placed there, as if for effect. It was at once ugly and beautiful, and defiantly both. As if it dared anyone who might enter to question its claim as a relic of a forgotten world.

"We probably ought to have it removed from the house as it has so continually been in disuse. It's from the early days of the estate when the area was far more sparsely populated. The family didn't like always having to travel to the church some distance, so they had a small little chapel built on to the side of the house here. For christenings and that sort of thing. You used to be able to access it from inside the house as well, so it was convenient when the weather was terrible. The door's still there, of course, though locked and I believe sealed but who knows. As you can see, they have just left this outside bit to return to nature. Graham tells me when he was a small child, he played in there very often, making up adventures and that sort of thing."

"It's a fascinating piece of architecture, and I like what age has done to it. It might be something useful we can use in the design of this area of the lawn. Maybe incorporate it in a grander pattern of planting or something."

"I could see it. I think Graham would appreciate that very much."

They went on walking down the hill until they came to the back lawns, portions of which Jonas had studied from his bedroom window. They talked of all the various plants taking over everything and the small stone walls that had been built to demarcate the different areas.

"So without sophistication and a bit depressing, I think," said Vita. "Downright Elizabethan, my mother-in-law calls it."

Jonas was drawn to walk over to the far edge of the lawn, just where the trees began. He gazed into the wood and saw something.

"Ah, so there is a cottage," he proclaimed.

Vita came up beside.

"Yes, a cottage. Is that particularly interesting? There are many about on the estate."

"No, not particularly," he confessed. "But yesterday, as I was standing by my window, I thought I saw activity here. But the rain and the gloom so obscured my vision, I could not exactly make out what it was."

Vita gave him a curious look. "You're rather one for peering out of windows, aren't you?"

Jonas felt pointed out.

"I suppose I am; that must seem rather rude. It's just that I am always looking to the landscape, I guess you might say. It is where my eye is drawn, always trying to figure out how nature and man meet."

Vita gave a small smile. "Not rude, I don't think. Curiosity is always healthy, I believe. Anyway, that cottage belongs to Patrick, the head groom. So you probably just noticed him coming home or something to that effect."

"Ah, yes, Patrick. We met him when we arrived. I'm sure that was it entirely. It makes perfect sense."

They moved back to the main part of the garden, studying the overgrown benches, the cracked paving stones. They stood before a fountain that had been claimed by age and neglect. Great vines of vegetation entwined the main tower of the fountain, their tendrils violently wrapped around the statue of the angel at the top, blossoms of color along their length blocking all but one eye of her stone face.

"So you expect Lord Stanley before dinner then?" asked Jonas as they studied it.

"Actually, no," said Vita. "It may be another day or so."

"Has anything happened?"

"Nothing so serious, I shouldn't think, or he might have said." She began walking back in the direction of the main house. "Patrick and I rode into the village early this morning and stopped at the post office. There was a telegram waiting from Graham to say he had been further delayed."

"I see."

He was beginning to feel rather used, and the thought gnawed at him. Somehow he felt as if he were here, not in the capacity promised, but as some sort of entertainment. Was he here only to provide distraction for a bored household of ladies?

"Are you too terribly annoyed?" Vita asked.

"I might ask the same of you, Lady Stanley," he snapped. "Aren't you too terribly annoyed? This constant back and forth, of waiting for your husband and never knowing exactly when he will show up? It feels rather like some constant game of cards. I can't imagine why you endure it."

Jonas dropped his head, surprised by his own vehemence, and cracked his knuckles. When he glanced at Vita, she seemed rather taken aback. "I apologize," he said, in a calm tone. "That was untoward of me and certainly none of my business."

She considered him. "No, no," she said. "Not to worry. Graham said you were rather prone to fits of passion."

"Graham said?" It was Jonas's turn to look taken aback. "I wasn't aware Lord Stanley had intimate knowledge of my temperament."

"He doesn't, of course, merely by reputation. Derrick has shared a story or two during their visits, I imagine. Who knows what men get up to with their port and cigars after dinner?"

Jonas was silent for a moment. He had failed to consider Derrick's intimacy with the family. What picture of Jonas had Derrick painted for them exactly? Did Lord Stanley have some sort of apprehension about him, is that why he delayed his arrival so?

"To answer your question," Vita said, interrupting his ruminating. "My husband's being absent does not irritate me because I find so much else to do."

"Like your horses?"

"Yes, like my horses." She laughed to herself. "Oh, Mister Laurence, you don't see only the surface of things, do you? Graham mentioned that as well."

Jonas tried to discern what she might alluding to with regard to the things about him which had been previously mentioned. It certainly seemed as if a decision of some sort had already been made about what type of person he was.

"It is, I'm afraid," he said, "the product of a restless mind. I am not quite used to being so alone with only my thoughts."

"I've grown rather fond of being alone with my thoughts, I must confess," said Vita.

"And it doesn't cause you any sort of resentment then?" Jonas asked. He thought of Pearson, sitting in the apartment in London, alone.

Vita laughed, surprising him.

"Resentment? Not at all. You see, Jonas, my husband and I have been the very closest friends for much of our lives. Even before we were married. Neither of us made an extraordinary amount of friends in our society, I'm afraid we both found most of them rather dull and, frankly, quite unintelligent. It sounds rather snobbish, I imagine, but it's true. I think you could probably understand."

He dropped his chin in concession.

"We always stayed close to one another weekend parties and social occasions," she continued. "So it seemed rather inevitable that we should end up together; everyone assumed we would. Our families, our mothers, who were such close friends as well. And so we did. It made sense, and it worked well for both families, emotionally as well as financially. I would never get Narrowend, our family estate, not with three brothers and numerous cousins. And I couldn't see myself fitting in with most of the other homes or families I'd known. So Hillcomb made sense. And my family, though more newly rich than the Stanleys, had the means to provide me quite a terrific dowry and allowance. So it's allowed us slowly but determinedly to make this into the estate we want. "

They had come to the top of the hill on the other side of the house. She turned, her gaze sweeping back over the grounds.

"Of course, Graham and I discussed all of this prior to marriage. We determined our boundaries, and knew that we both have very separate... interests, if you will." She gave him a curious look. "As well as many similar interests."

Jonas nodded, glad not to have offended her. More than anything, he was rather fascinated. They—the entire family—were very much originals, not like others he had met. On the surface, they seemed no different, really, but their attitudes were wholly of another set of values. Values he liked, he had to admit.

"It all seems extraordinarily modern, I must say," he finally said.

"We should take that very much as a compliment, I assure you."

Back inside, she offered him a drink in the study, taking one herself.

"It is a sizable estate you have," Jonas said. "Are there any neighbors to speak of?

"We have neighbors," answered Vita, sitting back on the leather armchair, "but they are hardly worth speaking of. Barnaby Manor, just on the other side of the lake there—the Cheering family. Can you imagine? As if any family name could be less aptly given. We are polite, of course, and do all the things expected, the usual visits at holidays and all that. But it has all been very strained since the falling out."

"The falling out?"

"Yes, with Nicholas, the eldest son. He was one of our few true friends growing up—Graham, Nicholas, and I. If anyone was to be our third amongst all those we knew, he was the one. He and Graham were especially close."

"But?"

"In the end, Nicholas grew up to be little more than a man of expectations. Not even a man, really, if you ask me, just a large child who hasn't the conviction or courage to be his own self. Only to listen to what his parents wanted from him."

"In my experience, that doesn't sound so highly unusual."

"No, I suppose not, but it was hard on Graham particularly. Nicholas handled it very badly—they had a bond those two, and Nicholas destroyed it. Callously." She sighed. "Perhaps it was the only way he knew how to handle it. But it was not the right way."

She got up and refilled her glass. "Anyway, Nicholas was very jovial at our wedding, even if the sentiment was not so readily returned. And he sent a lovely gift to the new baby. So I suppose he isn't all bad."

Jonas contemplated this. For some reason, he found her nonchalance rather irritating. He thought of his days in the city, among his business associates and the so-called social elite, and how often he felt on-guard. As if he had to monitor exactly what he said, how he said it, and about whom he said it. The enormous strain put on certain relationships—in fact, it was a concern which weighed on his relationship with Pearson quite heavily. This idea that they must always present a certain version of themselves to the world at large; whether it be Pearson pretending to be his valet on his client visits or pretending to be a butler or secretary at home when anyone outside of their circle of friends visited. And all in the name of maintaining the "proper" immutable order of things; all in the name of not casting oneself outside of the bounds of society through impropriety. And yet here, amongst the classes which defined society and its mores, they lived without regard. As if these things, these things which sometimes consumed his every social interaction in his daily life, were mere frivolities, to be ignored whenever it suited their wants and desires.

"I must say," he finally said. "You're awfully more open than most families I've met. So many I've encountered keep up pretenses even when those pretenses are blindingly transparent to all who look on them. And yet you speak so freely. I can't say it isn't a bit disconcerting."

"I hope you don't find us scandalous."

"Scandalous is not the word I would use exactly," he said gruffly.

Vita laughed at that.

Jonas went to refill his glass and then moved to the window to gaze out. How verdant it all looked in daylight, the undulating lawns, the full and heavy trees. A promise of something good and exciting. But in his mind was the idea that just around the corner, as it were, just on the other side there stuck out a crumbling, ill-formed chapel. Which, although it was covered in overgrown greenery that pulled at it to bring it back down to the earth, stood strong, irregular, obtuse, and proudly ugly. It was as if the estate offered him this challenge, that no matter how he might apply his designs and rituals of beautification, he would not fully escape the underneath, which was jagged and precarious.

"I hope you don't find me too terribly gauche," Vita continued. "But I will say it is not everyone with whom I let free my tongue so easily. You move me, Jonas Laurence. I cannot say why exactly but you do. Somehow you fit in this place. You feel like an odd piece of the puzzle that no one is able to locate and whose edges are cut in such a way as they won't seem to match, and yet a piece which slips easily into the missing spot. I admit we are unusual here in our own individual ways. But I think you are unusual too—in possibly quite the same manner as we are. Does that make any sense?"

Jonas was not sure how he felt being summed up so. What she said made sense, and, truthfully, he was glad she saw such a kinship in him. He had to admit that he felt much the same way about her and the other ladies—a loose freedom of being that he rarely encountered. But he wasn't sure he appreciated that the façade he worked so hard to construct could be so easily gotten past. Still, he shouldn't act with hastily. After all, he was here to do a job of work, and it was indeed a splendid place, a splendid mound of clay, if one might, offered to him to mold into a thing resplendent.

"There is something about the land itself which does make me feel as if I should be here," he said. "It is willed with a drama—an organic majesty—that inspires me. When I look out on the gardens, my mind is filled with ideas: some quite stunning and some, quite frankly, seem almost horrific in scale and measure. With most estates, I can come in and plan—I can divide the space in my mind and see it filled with exact measurements and elements. Fruits trees here, for their blossoms and their scent, a bed of flowers here for color and their language of symbolism, hedgerows there for definition, symmetry, and delineation. But here, at Hillcomb, I feel stories rather than see designs. And these stories seem to flow all over—to tumble over themselves, to overtake and envelop the place. I could be standing at the top of the hill with you just now and it is a symphony and then we turn a corner and, suddenly and unexpectedly, cacophony. It is unsettling and yet utterly thrilling. It's a challenge that I look forward to."

Vita stood and crossed to the drinks cabinet.

"Goodness, you speak so passionately of your work. It is encouraging and exciting. I know you and Graham will have much to talk about."

He rolled his eyes and turned towards her.

"Forgive me, your ladyship—Vita—but you sometimes speak as if Graham and I are already old friends. I don't usually think of my work as a social call, or as secondary to some other scheme. It is what I am passionate about, and, if I might, what sustains me—not only spiritually but financially. So while I do look forward to meeting Lord Stanley—should he ever actually materialize—I'm afraid I am not here primarily for his amusement or distraction."

Vita, frozen in the middle of refreshing her glass, looked abashed.

"I've offended you, Mister Laurence. I apologize."

"Not at all," said Jonas, feeling slightly ashamed at letting his annoyance break free so easily.

"It's only that in so many ways you remind me of my husband. And he is not a man that meets many with a like mind or similar outlook, so it strikes me. I do not mean to minimize your work."

"No, no, of course not. I think it was only that my mind is so jumbled. I'm anxious to get to work, for all the reasons I mentioned, and I fear I get rather irritable when I am left still for too long."

"I completely understand. I too need constant stimulation. Thank goodness for my stables. Now, shall we have lunch then? As it's just the two of us, I've asked Cook for something easy. Cold meats and salad, that sort of thing."

"I think I may pass, if you don't mind. I am eager to put some of my thoughts down on paper. But Lady Aldrange mentioned there might be some sketches for me?"

"Yes, of course," said Vita. "I hope they are of some help in your planning. I imagine they are more fanciful than instructive but Mamma couldn't wait to show them off. She's actually quite good, you know. If she had pursued training with any vigor I think she may have amounted to a real artist."

"What held her back then?" asked Jonas.

Vita looked at him in surprise. "Why, she got married, of course," said Vita brightly.

Chapter Six

A s Jonas opened the door to his room, he heard what sounded like a shuffling. He found Cecil standing next to the writing desk, brushing a hat that belonged to Jonas. He looked up from his work and smiled warmly. Perhaps a bit too warmly, in fact. A scamp, Jonas reminded himself.

"Hello, Cecil, I didn't expect to see you here just now."

"I've come to dress you for dinner, haven't I, sir."

Jonas approached the desk. He laid the watercolors on its surface and retrieved his diary from the corner where he'd left it earlier. He removed the pen shoved inside as a place marker, and clicked the lock on the journal shut. He placed it on top of the watercolors and pushed them all to the back of the desk.

"You do realize, Cecil, that dinner isn't for hours yet?"

Cecil nodded, handing Jonas the brushed hat.

"I didn't expect you to be back so soon yourself," said Cecil. "I thought you was having luncheon with her ladyship."

Jonas laid the hat on the desk and cut his eye at Cecil. "I wasn't much in the mood for eating."

Cecil stepped closer. "Did you miss me last night, sir?"

"Is that why you've come, Cecil? To apologize for last night?"

Cecil scoffed. "I don't have anything to apologize for, Mister Laurence."

"No, of course not. The butler called you on an errand, and you have your duties to attend to."

"Avery didn't call on me for nothing," countered Cecil with a smirk. "That's just what I told Sarah, ain't it."

Jonas felt stupid for the prick of pain that caused him. It was ridiculous, of course, but he was forced to admit, he had been looking forward to the company of a man last night. Despite his bizarre dream, he still felt unsatisfied, in need of real touch, skin on skin, and the warmth of a body against his own.

"So you changed your mind about visiting me then?" he asked, hoping none of his emotions shone through in his voice.

Cecil shrugged. "I wouldn't say that, exactly, sir. But I can decide what to do with my nights, can't I? I'm not at your beck and call every minute of the day, to do with as you wish when you wish. I reckon I am allowed to entertain myself how I see fit, regardless of what you say."

Jonas felt rather bad suddenly. Perhaps he had grown too accustomed to playing the role of the aristocrat. Who was he to make demands of a man who had been assigned to him as a job?

"Of course, I didn't mean that at all, Cecil. I only meant—oh bugger, what does it matter?" He turned towards the desk. "Thank you for the hat, but I'll just write for now if you don't mind."

"Now, sir, don't be hasty, sir." Cecil pulled him closer. "It weren't my intention to get you bothered. But you are rather astonishing when you get fiery."

Cecil moved in very closely and licked his lips. "I'm glad to see that you missed me, though."

"Did I say that?" asked Jonas.

Cecil adjusted the lapels of Jonas's jacket, letting his hands slide down, resting at the hips. Jonas noticed a smile creeping onto Cecil's lips. As coquettish as it may have been, the man certainly knew how to play the part well.

"I don't often get to serve guests the likes of you, sir." Cecil rubbed his hand over Jonas's crotch and gave it a squeeze. Jonas gasped. "I very much wouldn't want to disappoint you."

Cecil kissed him then, quite passionately. Tongue teasing, his mouth firm and aggressive then slack and beckoning. He broke away. "You know, I have been told I am an exemplary valet, sir."

"Yes," said Jonas, "That I can well imagine."

Cecil knelt in front of him. "And I have a reputation to maintain. In my line of work, sir, reputation is everything."

He undid Jonas's trousers and slid his hand in to retrieve the stiffening cock. Jonas felt as if he ought to protest, but the touch was welcome beyond belief. There was something so familiar, and comforting about Cecil's hands on him. And he longed, even if for a few moments, to erase the noise clouding his mind. He gave in.

"Yes, well," said Jonas, "we wouldn't want to endanger your reputation, would we."

"No, sir," said Cecil, looking up at him with a wicked expression. "Thank you, sir."

Jonas closed his eyes, threw back his head, and prayed he didn't moan too loudly.

The after-dinner conversation that evening was quite lively. The Dowager Countess and Lady Aldrange had much to share about their afternoon in the village—all of the familiar faces they had encountered, all of the new shops they perused. And, of course, Lady Aldrange, dear Flora, wanted to know what he thought of her little colorful daubs, as she called them. Jonas was glad that he could quite truthfully compliment her eye and talent. This led to a discussion of what he had thought of the garden in general, and did he think he could do something—*anything, really*, said the Dowager Countess—with it. He assured the ladies he was convinced he could, and he was hopeful of corralling the color and vibrancy of the local plant life to make something picturesque of the grounds. He had a vague idea of pergolas covered in wisteria or roses, and, perhaps, a shady loggia where the ladies might take their tea.

As Lady Aldrange pressed the back of her hand to her mouth to stifle a yawn, Jonas realized that Vita was no longer with them.

"It has been quite a long day," said the Dowager Countess. "We are very much ready for bed, I should think."

"I can't imagine where Vita has gotten to," said Lady Aldrange, "but do stay and have a drink if you like."

"I thank you ladies," said Jonas, "but I believe I have had quite enough to drink of late. I think I shall retrieve something to read from the library and then follow your example."

He escorted the duo to the stairwell where he left them.

When he reached the doorway to the library, he was surprised to find Vita alone there. She stood in the very same window in which he had the night before as he spied upon the curious folly.

"Oh, I'm sorry," he said. "Didn't mean to disturb you."

Vita turned with a start but immediately regained herself. "Jonas, not at all. You're not disturbing me." She saw his hand move towards the light switch. "No, please don't turn on the light yet. I came in to fetch a book and I noticed the way the moonlight was falling on the trees just outside. It was especially beautiful. It sounds silly, I know."

She turned back to the window, and he came up beside her.

"It is especially magical," he agreed. "I noticed the very same myself last night."

"Last night?" She kept her gaze turned outside. "So you did visit the library last night then?"

"Yes, as you suggested. Just before I went to bed, I came to see if I could find anything interesting."

She turned to him. "And did you? Find anything interesting, I mean."

He felt as if beneath her question, there lay a test of some sort.

"Something, I thought, at first," he replied. "But it didn't turn out to be much."

She nodded, turning her gaze back outside. She seemed intent, as if searching for something. A signal perhaps? Jonas wondered.

"I am sorry about my husband being so much delayed. Do you mind rattling around here with us all these empty hours?"

Jonas stood beside her, his gaze landing on the folly in the woods.

"Isn't it odd," he said, "how things can seem so attractive, even paramountly so, when we first encounter them? How they can seem to fill out all the niches we thought unfilled and smooth all the edges left rough? But despite their initial promise, how they can leave us feeling just as empty as we ever did?"

Vita turned her face to him. Her eyes were narrowed slightly and her expression was questioning—challenging even.

"In truth," he said, turning away from her and the window with a sigh, "I have no desire to rush back to London. I had left these next few days free to deal with.... With any unfinished business that might present itself."

"That's good then isn't it," she said vaguely.

"Yes, I suppose so. Should you find me a good match I will be able to devote myself to the plans for Hillcomb for some days."

"I have no doubt of your being a match," said Vita. "Though the final decision belongs to Graham, of course, I anticipate his wants will be met."

She leaned forward, resting her palms on the windowsill.

"Have you checked in on your man, Donaldson?" she asked. "I'm sure our staff have made him quite comfortable, but it isn't good for anyone to feel neglected, no matter their station. I think everyone who provides something for us should be given the full devotion of our attention. Don't you agree, Jonas?"

Her face was a mask. He felt he was being politely ushered on. But seeing a familiar face like Donaldson's would serve him well just now.

"Yes, I do agree. That's quite a good idea, actually. I'll leave you in peace then," he said. "Shall I turn on the light as I leave?"

"No, don't bother, if you don't mind."

"Not at all. Goodnight then, Vita."

"Goodnight."

After some stumbling into various rooms and stairwells along with some lucky guesswork, Jonas located the stairs to the servants' hall and descended. Even before he reached the bottom of the stairwell, he felt a welcome humor overwhelm him. From below there was warmth, no doubt the kitchen fires filling the hall, and much convivial chatter and even, if he wasn't mistaken, the soft trills of a lovely singing voice somewhere. It seemed the servants' hall of this house was a world away from the upstairs chambers, with their austerity and emptiness.

It was hard to imagine, as he stepped down into the hall and surveyed the lively scene, that this was the same house. A young maid nearby spied him and gasped and at once all the noise ceased and heads turned his way.

"Oh, don't mind him, you lot," he heard Donaldson's voice ring out. "That's just Mister Laurence. You needn't stifle yourselves for him, he's a good sort. Not one of your toffee-nosed crowd."

Jonas found Donaldson by following his voice and saw him sitting in a comfortable-looking chair, with a woman, a kitchen maid it seemed by her apron and outfit, sitting quite close by and pretending not to look adoringly at him. Jonas smiled. Donaldson, if no one else, had certainly adjusted quite well to the temporary digs.

"Yes, yes, please," called out Jonas as he found himself reverting to the accent of his youth. "Don't mind me. Keep on with your good time; it makes me quite jolly to see. I've just come to talk to my man Donaldson is all."

The servants seemed wary but the conversation started back up, without, Jonas was disappointed to notice, the singing. As Donaldson approached him, Jonas was struck by the notion that he had no real reason to be paying a visit to his chauffeur at such an hour. But as he glanced around at the snug comfort of the servants' hall, he was gladdened by the atmosphere. And, too, it delayed another inevitable confrontation with that terrible, disturbing picture.

"Hello, sir," Donaldson said.

"Hello there, Donaldson. You seem to be getting along quite nicely."

Donaldson glanced back at the hall.

"I suppose so, sir. I reckon I've learned to make myself at home anywhere, what with all our travels."

"Yes, I see," Jonas said blandly.

Donaldson eyed him.

"Was there something I could help you with, sir?" he asked.

A kernel of a thought came to Jonas and he went with it.

"Actually, yes," he said. "I had a book with me when we arrived, *Gifts for the Sheikh*, and I can't seem to locate it in my belongings upstairs. I wondered if you had encountered it, possibly left in the car."

Donaldson considered. "No, sir. I've not seen any book. But I will keep my eye out for it."

"Yes, do, Donaldson, there's a good man. If you see it anywhere, claim it. It's not a book for all eyes, if you catch my meaning," Jonas offered cautiously.

"Aye, sir, not for the eyes of young maids and that?" Donaldson said with a grin.

"Yes, exactly."

There was a moment of awkward silence and Jonas began to turn to head back upstairs. "Yes, well, thank you, Donaldson. I'll leave you to it then."

"Sir. I wondered," Donaldson began. "Well, sir, is everything all right then? I mean, with you."

Jonas turned back to him.

"All right? Why shouldn't I be all right, Donaldson?"

Donaldson scratched his chin and glanced over his shoulder. "Only Patrick—the Head Groom, that is—said he heard strange noises coming from your hallway last night, just around midnight. And I reckon I wondered if you were ill or something."

Jonas thought back to his disconcerting dream. Had he cried out in his sleep? He cleared his throat.

"Strange noises?" he asked, hoping he wasn't blushing. "What sort of strange noises?"

"I'm not sure, sir. But he said sounded as if they might be some sort of struggle or scuffle afoot."

"Is that so?" Jonas wasn't sure how to reply, so instead, he evaded response. "What was Patrick doing upstairs around midnight? It seems an odd hour for a stablemaster to be needed."

"I'm sure I couldn't say, sir," Donaldson said quickly. "I only ask, sir, because they do say there are odd things that happen in that room."

"'Odd things'?"

"Yes, sir. One of the maids was telling me that strange, queer things have befallen guests what stayed in that room. It has a history, you see. It seems some guests have been troubled by the place."

"What sort of history is that?"

"I couldn't exactly say, sir. They were rather vague, these tellings. But they say Lord Stanley insists that no guests stay in that room. That is, not usually, sir. They seem to think there might be something meaningful—that is, well, how do you say, something doomed about someone staying there."

Jonas tried to fight off the shiver the man's words gave him. They seemed to play into the sense of foreboding he had felt all evening. He couldn't help but wonder if his being put in that room was yet another test from his hosts. Why had they chosen this specific room, one which inspired so chatter and gossip among the staff?

He cleared his throat.

"Well, Donaldson, you know how they can be in the country sometimes, especially as unto themselves as they are here. Stories, superstitions, all of that sort of thing. Sometimes it makes a day of chores go by faster to think there might be spirits afoot than to accept that a room is, inevitably, just a room."

Donaldson raised his brows. "Yes, sir. If you say so, sir."

"I do, indeed." Jonas took a step up. "Goodnight, then, Donaldson."

Donaldson touched his forehead as if tipping his usual cap. "Goodnight, sir."

Back in the dreary dark of the upstairs world, Jonas headed for the stairwell. As he stepped up, he stared at the dreaded portrait that had become his nemesis. At every encounter, it seemed to look different to him—and differently *at* him. Tonight, it had managed its most dramatic stance yet. On either side of the landing, the two tables held lit lamps. Three lit lamps were burning on the table. One per person, he should imagine, so there ought to be only two left. Of course, the Dowager Countess and Lady Aldrange likely shared a lamp, so it appeared Vita still had not yet come upstairs.

He lifted his head toward the painting, now glowing warmly from the low lit wicks, and scowled at it. The whole scene felt like some altar to a pagan god or like some welcoming shrine to the Devil himself at the entrance of Hell. Jonas stalked up the stairs and stared into the eyes of the figure in the portrait. The man seemed to be laughing at him. The damned thing had gotten him into such a state that he was breathing heavily, his whole body tingling. He took up one of the lamps and moved closer, touching its surface. Nothing. Nothing but canvas and dried oils, the brushstrokes thick and rough. Nothing more. As to be expected.

Below him, somewhere a door slammed loudly, and he spun around. He could see no one below and there was no further noise. Still his nerves felt frayed.

Turning back, he felt the painting menacing above him. He narrowed his eyes at the smirking countenance.

It's a good thing I'm not an architect, he thought, *or else I would remove this creature immediately*.

"And how would you like that?" he said out loud in a blustery tone. Then he caught himself, feeling stupid to being confronting a blasted painting.

"Enough," he said under his breath. This was all just stuff and nonsense and noise in his head.

He peered down the long, cold hallway heading to his room and irritation rose up in him. If only it could be like the servants' hall, warm and welcoming, instead of being so cold and creepy and empty with loneliness. Throwing the portrait one last look of disgust, he went on his way.

His irritation still piqued, Jonas was not placated by the sight of Cecil lying on his bed in wait. Cecil had removed his jacket and shoes and undone his shirt so that the undershirt highlighted his well-defined chest, the soft curls peeking out just at the top. He seemed extremely comfortable there.

He was smiling up at Jonas with a hazy expression, drunk he seemed, on wine or lust, Jonas couldn't be sure.

"Isn't this all just a little too familiar?" snapped Jonas.

As the fire was burning bright, he took the lamp to the mantle and lowered the wick to extinguish it.

"What's the matter?" asked Cecil. "I thought you enjoyed this afternoon."

"And if I did?" Jonas leaned against the mantel-piece massaging the bridge of his nose.

"I reckoned we might have some more this evening."

Although he knew Cecil was trying to soothe him, he couldn't quite shake his irritation. Had this scene occurred last night as planned, he wouldn't have been subjected to that terrible dream that had left him open for humiliation and speculation. His eyes shot to the bedside table.

"No tea this evening then?" he asked abruptly.

Cecil sat up in the bed and moved to the edge.

"Tea?" His face softened. He looked so surprised, so innocent. So dangerously beautiful.

"Last night you left me tea, did you not?" Jonas asked, his voice softening a bit.

"I didn't bring any tea, sir. That'll be Sarah."

"And she says she did not."

Cecil smiled and shook his head. "Sarah doesn't have all the straw in her mattress, sir. A few ribbons short of a bonnet if you get my meaning."

He got up and moved towards Jonas who sighed heavily.

"There are far too many games being played in this household," he said.

"There are no games here now. No mystery," said Cecil. He began to loosen Jonas's tie and massage his shoulders. "And you shan't need any tea tonight. I shall personally make sure you are quite relaxed."

He kissed Jonas on the lips, but Jonas pushed him back.

"I'm afraid I'm not in the mood just now," said Jonas.

Cecil gave him a mock pout. "I'm afraid I am in the mood though, sir. Give us a kiss then. All you need is to relax." He pressed himself against Jonas and moved his mouth.

Jonas turned his head.

"Are we sure you don't like games then, sir?" asked Cecil. "Who's the one being a tease then now?"

"I assure you, I do not mean to a tease," Jonas insisted. "I am just not very much in want of company."

Cecil grabbed his chin roughly and tried to turn his head for another kiss, but Jonas shook loose his grip. Cecil pushed himself back from the mantle and gave Jonas a pitying look.

"Oh, yes, you and his lordship should get along quite nicely then," he said, his voice sharp like a blade. "Two peas in a pod, I should say."

Jonas shook his head. What had Lord Stanley to do with this? Always this man's name, popping up in conversation like some specter of the recently departed.

"I beg your pardon?"

Cecil gave a quick grunt of a laugh as he retrieved the pieces of his livery he had earlier discarded. "He doesn't have much backbone either, Mister Graham Grey."

"Backbone? What is that supposed to mean exactly?" snapped Jonas.

"You'll pardon me, sir," answered Cecil, "but you act like you want one thing and then suddenly act as if you don't. Or is it that have you gotten what use you needed of me, sir? And now you're done?"

Jonas straightened and took a step forward. "I think you're taking this a bit far, don't you, Cecil? I intended no such insinuation."

Cecil tutted. "Nothing to worry your pretty little head over, sir. Not for old Cecil, no. I've gotten what use I needed as well." He paused and let his eyes rake up and down Jonas's body. "Just about, that is, sir. Just about."

"Now, look here, Cecil."

But Cecil was at the servants' passage panel already, opening. He turned and gave Jonas an exaggerated bow.

"Sweet dreams, Mister Laurence, sir."

Jonas stood for a moment, dumbfounded. He was shocked at how quickly the young man's mood had turned black. He had only wanted to be left alone; he had not intended to offend Cecil. The young man did not take well to not calling the shots; that much was evident. Maybe, in their short acquaintance, Cecil had formed a stronger bond to him than Jonas realized. The sudden turn of mood suggested some deep-seated issues. Maybe he could sort it out in the morning, make Cecil understand that it was only frayed nerves, not a want to dismiss him entirely.

He glanced over at the small desk and his diary there. Maybe he ought to put it all out on paper; that usually helped him to make sense of what he felt. But he shook his head. Not now, not tonight. The last thing he wanted right now was to get lost in his own head even more. Sleep is what he needed; sleep is what he lacked. Last night had not been restful and he blamed it for his clouded mental fog now.

He would change for bed and welcome the rest.

Chapter Seven

J onas awoke with a strangling gasp from a dream filled with devilish eyes, handsome faces, the smell of oil paint, and the lick of flames. He snatched his head around. Had he heard a noise when he woke? He felt as if something had signaled to him to wake up, a presence in the room. But the room was dark and seemingly empty. He had no idea how long he had slept. The fire had died down to mere embers, and Jonas felt a chill. The bedclothes offered little protection against the cold, so he got out of bed, heading towards the wardrobe near the window where he remembered seeing a quilt stored in the bottom.

It was storming again, Jonas thought as he heard the thunder rumble outside. It instantly sounded again, without pause, and listening more closely, he realized that what he thought was thunder was the bark of dogs. Several of them bellowing out to one another. He passed the window and his eye fell onto the glass. Shaking his head, he thought to turn away, refusing to be caught up yet again in this game of shadows. Except that he had detected hurried movement out of the corner of his eye, something like the form and shape of a person, and curiosity got the best of him.

The figure moved into view, and it was indeed a man. A man in trousers and a waistcoat, strolling through the garden. Patrick, the groomsman, Jonas thought with a nod, returning to his cottage. Only then the man paused and lifted his arms signaling two hounds, and then a third, to approach and circle him, their barks sounding even through the window glass. He dropped his arms and dogs were sprinting off again. The mysterious man turned back in the direction of the house. He lifted his head and looked directly at Jonas's window. The moonlight fell across his face, and Jonas gasped, drawing in a deep breath of disbelief. There, standing in the garden, was the man from the painting, the former Lord Stanley with the devilish eyes. Jonas shook his head, refusing to accept what his mind told him. The man smiled then, and nodded at him, still watching the window. Jonas stumbled back from the window, shocked to be acknowledged. He rubbed his eyes.

"Rubbish," he said out loud. "Impossible."

He scolded himself. A man decades dead could not be walking around the grounds. It was must be Patrick, and his exhausted mind was only playing tricks on him yet again. He refused to believe it. But he felt compelled to steal another glance; just to be sure.

Back at the window, he saw nothing, no one. *There, you see*, he told himself, *tricks of the mind, that's all*. But then the dogs came dashing back into view, and the man emerged again, passing from behind one of the large misshapen shrubs. He was closer to the house now. Jonas watched him, trying to steal a glimpse of his face. Trying to convince himself that he could not have seen what he thought he had seen. When the man was but a few yards away, he stopped and looked up again—directly at Jonas. They held one another's gaze. The face staring back at him was the one from the portrait, without a doubt. Jonas thought he might faint and put a hand on the glass to steady himself. The ghost, as Jonas had already accepted he must be, seemed to react to this motion. He nodded and lifted his own hand as if returning a wave. Jonas blinked, shocked, and dropped his hand, backing away from the window.

Compelled, he lurched towards the glass but the man was gone.

"No," hissed Jonas. "No more games."

He tore out of the room, pausing only by the door to grab a pair of shoes, those he had worn to dinner, and flew into the hallway.

He dashed down the stairs, not pausing to look at that accursed painting. As he reached the bottom of the stairs, he lost his footing and fell onto the floor. Pushing himself back up, he spun toward the portrait. No light fell on it now, but the outlines of the face could be made out, even in the shadows, and he swore the eyes sparkled, no doubt laughing at him and cursing him for the ridiculous creature that he was.

"Damn you," he swore under his breath.

And then the sound of muted laughter from somewhere.

He was on his feet in an instant.

The laughter echoed, and then stopped, the space left hollow in its sudden silence.

"Who's there?" he called out.

The only answer he received was the howling and barking of the hounds from some distant place on the grounds. He rushed for the front door, determined to find this phantom, and confront it. He must make this nonsense end. Pushing out the door, he found himself in the *porte-cochère* unsure of which way to go. He thought he heard movement, footsteps on the crushed shell, and then howls of the dogs again, coming from the east of the house. He took off.

Rounding the side of the house, he saw no one and heard no dogs. The air was drier than before, crisp as in those moments just before a storm, where the wind swirls and the clouds gather all their moisture to set free a torrent. As if to confirm his suspicion, he heard a roll of thunder far off in the distance, followed by a crack of lightning. It was not a close bolt but it was enough to illuminate the nearest trees momentarily and he saw the outline of the folly. The sound of the dogs flared up again, coming from which direction he could not discern.

He scrambled down the hill, passing the chapel, but the darkness had made him forget how steep its incline. Suddenly he was falling, tumbling down the hill. He felt his knee hit a rock, and it tore through the thin fabric of the nightshirt. He was too shocked to cry out, and before he realized what was happening, he landed with a thud at the bottom.

He threw himself to his feet and glanced around, trying to propel himself forward. But he was dizzy from the tumble, and fell backward, his rear meeting the ground.

What was he doing? Chasing a phantom in the middle of the night? Half-naked and half-awake, he had run out onto the grounds to do what exactly? Confront the ghost he swore he had seen from his bedroom window. The sheer delirium of it hit him then. He listened and heard no hounds, no barking, no howls. Not even the accursed shouts of those bloody foxes. All he heard was the approaching rumble of thunder. A new storm brewing and headed this way. He stared down as far as his sight would allow and saw the moonlight shimmering on the surface of the lake. He laid back on the ground feeling absurd and defeated.

Raindrops smacked against his face and he stood. His footing seemed steady despite the pain in his knee and so he set about moving back up the hill. The thunder crashed and the heavens opened, a deluge of water showering down on him. Slipping more than a few times, and almost tumbling again, he made it to the crest, just as the rain began to fall with even more force.

He was mere feet away from the chapel, and so ran to it, hoping its doors weren't boarded shut and that he could obtain momentary refuge from the elements.

As he pushed in, the thunder was loud and boomed across the sky. More crackling lightning followed and the rain advanced. The gusts that followed him in seemed to rush to the top of the high ceiling of the chapel and stir the cold air nestled there. He shivered and wrapped his arms about himself. Had he been a man of faith he might have taken the opportunity to pray for guidance or at least a break from precipitation. But as it were, he instead sought out somewhere to sit and rest for a moment. There were a few pews shoved to the side, some broken, some crumbling from rot, but one remained sturdy, and still faced the altar. It was all rather disturbing in the dark of night, and not at all reassuring, as he was told religion ought to be. Still, it was a refuge and he collapsed onto the pew, letting his body acknowledge the aches and cuts and scrapes he had just caused it.

He sat looking up at the great expanse behind the pulpit. It was just big enough, he thought, to house that blasted portrait from inside. Maybe someone ought to take it down and give it a new home here.

And then he heard it. The same eerie voice from the night before. That voice which had visited him in his dream.

"Jooooonassss."

The same voice that has shushed him when his limbs were frozen in place.

"Joonassss."

He froze. He was most certainly going mad. Of this, he was now convinced.

"Joooonassssssss."

Louder this time and with a sibilant ending. He jumped up.

"Who's there?" he demanded.

"Joooonasssssss."

It wasn't just his mind now; it couldn't be. Could it? No, a real voice was calling out, twisting his name.

"Who are you?" he called out. "Show yourself!"

There was a rumbling chuckle, deep and distant.

"I won't play these games," he bellowed.

"Joooonassss," the voice called.

"Enough!" he shouted and turned for the door.

"Laaarrrry," the voice increased in volume.

Jonas was rooted to the spot, unable to move.

"Laaarrrry Jo."

No one called him Larry Jo anymore. Only one person had ever called him by that pet name: Marcus. Marcus—his former lover; his dead lover. Jonas felt something come loose in his chest and his breathing came rapidly.

"Marcus?" he whispered. "Marcus, is that you? Can it be?"

He willed his feet to move, but they would not; his hands clenched and unclenched.

"Larrrrrrry Joooo," the voice repeated.

The voice seemed to have shifted to another part of the chapel. Jonas spun around, trying to find its source.

"No!" he cried out. "Show yourself now!"

"Larry Joooooo why did you leave him too?"

"What?" cried Jonas. "Who?"

"Peeeeearson! You left him just like you left me!"

A roll of thunder outside.

"I didn't leave anyone!" yelled Jonas.

"YOU DID! ADMIT IT!" the voice commanded. "You abandoned him too!"

Jonas threw his hands to his face and shook his head, fighting against the words. But somewhere in the back of his mind, the voice connected with truth. He had abandoned Pearson, just like he had abandoned Marcus so long before. Not in the same manner, but the result was the same. He had given Pearson years of his life. But in truth, what had Jonas truly given him? An echo of love; a charcoal sketch of a partner, devoid of color and dimension; that was all. During their time together, Jonas had constantly been fleeing, running away from emotions he dared not acknowledged, in search of something vague and just out of reach. He spent those years trying to fulfill a gnawing need of love, love of a depth he had never felt with Pearson. Love of a depth he had only felt once before—once before with Marcus.

"Leave me be!" shouted Jonas. "What kind of trickery is this? How do you know these names?"

He had had enough. Jonas turned towards the door.

"You killed his love!" The voice took on a shrill new quality, like a keening wind. "Just like you killed Marcus!"

Jonas came to a halt. He felt as if a dagger had been plunged into his chest. Good lord, what was going on? Had he lost complete control of his faculties? How could this be happening?

"I did not kill Marcus!" he railed against the phantom voice.

"YOU DID! ADMIT IT! If you had not broken his heart, he would never have gone to war!"

Jonas fell into the nearest broken pew. A sob, with the intensity of fire, burned in his chest. It was true, and it hurt too much to be believed. Marcus was the only person he had ever truly loved, but he could not accept Marcus's love, not fully, not in the way Marcus had wanted to give it, not then. It had been too much for Jonas. And so he rejected Marcus—pushed him from his life. He had never intended it to be forever. Somewhere deep in his mind, deep in his heart, he knew he would always go back to Marcus. When he could, when he was able. When he was prepared for that kind of love. But Marcus could not stand the hurt, and so he had left, throwing himself into the Boer War. Fighting like a madman, they said, tearing across the fields, hunting the enemy. And Jonas knew that the enemy he had hunted was actually him; that Marcus had warred against the heartbreak Jonas had left him with. Until there was nothing more, nothing left to fight. Until that day when Jonas received a letter from Marcus's sister saying that he had been killed in battle.

And Jonas, too, had been battling against this heartbreak. All these years he had been telling himself that there was something more, some kind of love just out of reach. A want he could not identify, a shadow he could not form into something real and concrete. But he did know, he had known all along, though he could not admit it to himself, that what he wanted was the type of love he shared with Marcus. He had settled ever since for fleeting satisfactions or for a love that resembled what he told himself he wanted. Even though he knew it could not reach the heights or dimensions of what his heart yearned for. In trying to deny the deep guilt he felt for what he had done to Marcus, in trying to convince himself that he was searching for something more, instead of accepting the anger he had for himself for letting it slip away, he had kept himself from truly loving anyone again. In trying to obfuscate the pain and remorse he carried as a result of his time with Marcus, he had kept his heart an object, a thing to be examined and commented on, to be written about in the pages of his diary and then locked away behind its metal clasp, rather than a real thing, beating, alive, and wanting.

The fire broke free and Jonas began to weep. Deep throbbing sobs that wracked his body, the pain of all those years buried so far below. He wailed and cried, he wanted to scream until the hurt faded. And although he was not sure the hurt would ever fade, his weeping did.

He fell back in the wooden pew, wrecked. He closed his eyes against the echoes of pain bouncing around inside his body.

But that relentless voice hissed afresh,

"Larrrrrrrry." The voice came softly through the darkness. This time it sounded like a question.

"No!" shouted Jonas. "No, no, no!" The fire of hurt was replaced with a new spark – anger. "Whoever you are— Whatever you are—leave me be! I won't listen to this insanity!"

And he ran, pushing open the doors of the chapel and falling onto the grass.

He was on his feet again and racing up the hill, stopping at the top to catch his breath. He peered back down at the chapel. He watched it, waiting, hoping for someone to emerge. Someone on whom he could pin this anger, someone he could blame for this hurt. But no one came.

He heard footsteps on the grass.

It was Patrick, the head groom, coming down the hill. Seeing Jonas there, Patrick began to walk faster, away from him.

"You there," Jonas cried out. "I say, aren't you Patrick?"

Patrick stopped in place, his head turned away.

"Where are you coming from?"

Patrick met his gaze then, those intense, wild eyes, fiery, even in the night. "What concern is it of yours?" he asked, his voice a blunted sword.

Jonas knew it was ridiculous, but he had to ask. "Were you just in the chapel?"

"The chapel?" Patrick stared at him dumbfounded. "Why the hell would I be in the chapel?"

"So that wasn't you then?"

"Wasn't me when?"

"And the hounds, were you the one shepherding the hounds?"

"Of course not." Patrick turned up his lip in disgust. "I don't fool with those bloody dirty beasts."

"But they were there, near your cottage, you must have seen them."

Patrick glanced over his shoulder at the house. "I have been otherwise occupied." He looked at Jonas with more compassion now. "Perhaps you ought to get inside, sir. You look like you've been caught in the rain, and unexpectedly at that. You ought not to be running around outside in your nightshirt. Some might begin to wonder after your health."

Jonas blinked and nodded. He was conscious of what an absolute tragedy he must present.

"Yes, he agreed, "some might." He stood straighter, his voice steadier than before. "My apologies for accosting you so. I assure you there is nothing the matter. Only this house...."

Patrick began to move again, walking past him. "Aye, sir. Hillcomb leaves many a man confused beyond accounting."

Coming in the front door of the house, Jonas looked up. The portrait was still obscured, shadowed in the dark. But he no longer cared. If the whole of the thing had sprung forth from its mounting and flown across the foyer to crush him, he would not have been surprised nor protested. He reached down and shucked off the leather shoes. He did not want to leave muddy footprints all through the house to raise more questions in the morning. All he wanted now was to get into his bed and sleep. As he climbed the stairs, he did not pause to check the devilish face.

Closing the bedroom door, he dropped the muddied shoes near the fire. The room was dark save for the dim moonlight falling through the window, the corners pitch black and obscured. He stepped towards the bed and halted. He felt something, some presence in the room. There was a scent he did not recognize, the way the air moved felt different. Was it Cecil, returned? He studied the darkened corner just past the window.

"Yes, then," he said in a weary voice. "Show yourself."

And from the dark shadow stepped the ghost.

He moved out of the blackness and into the light of the window so that his form and face were visible. That same mercilessly beautiful face from the portrait, the same nose, the same mouth, the same eyes, the same dancing gleam within them.

Jonas suddenly felt completely sober and alert.

"But...but...how is it possible? You can't be here," exclaimed Jonas

"But you summoned me." The ghost approached Jonas.

"Did I?"

Jonas felt the presence of the spirit him; he could feel the heat radiating from its body. A heat like the wicks of a thousand oil lamps, all burning at once. A heat that started small but that he knew would rage, like a fire, and consume him.

"I have waited for this moment ever since my eyes first fell on you," said the ghost. "I have studied you, you know."

"Yes. I know."

And Jonas did know. The appraising stares, the way his eyes had followed him wherever he was, the changes of expression, of mood, in the painting. He knew it had been him. It had not all been in his mind after all.

"I have been watching you, waiting for this moment," said the ghost. "For the right time. For when you were finally free, finally open to my desire."

He reached up and brushed his fingertips across Jonas's cheek. "Are you? Are you open now?"

"Oh yes," said Jonas, his voice a whisper that caught in the back of his throat, throttled by desire.

In his wild imaginings, he had expected this moment to be vicious, cruel, and frightening. He thought meeting the ghost would be the destruction of his soul. But there was something very familiar about the specter, something soft yet strong, like the yearning for a touch kept secret.

"No— No, I don't know..." Jonas began, but he shook his head, stopping himself.

He must truly have gone to the other side of sanity. But at this point he was weak. Maybe he would wake up and it would all have been a dream; maybe he would close his eyes and never wake again, his fevered mind havinggiven in to its fate. He was too tired to care, at this point. He had given up so much tonight. Bodily pain, soul pain. He felt empty and he needed to be filled. His body yearned for comfort; to be touched, to be held. He gave in.

"Yes," he confessed. "Yes, I do want you. But how? How can it be?"

"It isn't so strange as all that." The ghost stepped forward and caressed his neck. His hand was warm, not cold and flimsy as Jonas might have imagined. But as supple as if blood flowed through him. "I'm sure you're not unfamiliar. You only need tell me what you want from me."

"You can't be real," Jonas said, his voice shaking.

"I assure I am very much real," said the ghost.

He pressed his body against Jonas, and Jonas felt just how real he was.

Before Jonas could move, the ghost had laid his hands on Jonas's chest and pulled him in for a deep kiss. The kiss was warm, his tongue delightful, and Jonas opened his mouth to succumb to its demands. The ghost hummed a small sound of approval and Jonas felt his body acquiesce.

"You smell like the gardens," whispered Jonas.

The ghost laughed. "Do I?"

"Yes, like rich, wet earth."

The ghost kissed his neck.

"And flowers," said Jonas.

The ghost moved his mouth up until he reached an earlobe which he sucked softly.

"Like honeysuckle and roses."

The ghost licked his collarbone.

"Like leaves and grass," gasped Jonas.

The ghost hands moved his hands around, caressing Jonas's lower back.

"You smell of the trees," Jonas murmured, nuzzling kisses into the ghost's neck.

The ghost grabbed Jonas's ass, caressing it, his fingers clutching onto its curves. Jonas nibbled on the ghost's bottom lip, letting his tongue caress its lines.

"You taste of rain," he whispered.

A crack of lightning lit the room for a brief moment, and then thunder roared outside, so loudly it shook the windowpane. The storm was unleashed.

The ghost reached down, and in one fluid motion pulled the nightshirt up and off of Jonas's body. Jonas moved his hand over the lines and muscles of the ghost's form, finding the buttons and ties, and divesting him of any material covering him until they both stood there together, naked in the moonlight.

"But this is impossible," Jonas said.

"Is it?" asked the ghost. His hand slid down and clutched Jonas's erect cock. "This feels very possible indeed."

Jonas let out a small moan at the contact.

"Tell me what you want," said the ghost, moving his hand back and forth, stroking Jonas. He moved Jonas's hand so that he might return the caress.

Jonas reveled in the touch of his perfect skin, his perfect body, its lines and angles just like his face, carved as if from the hands of an artist.

"I need," began Jonas, "I need to be filled up. I am so empty."

The ghost stepped forward, taking his mouth. And then they were on the bed, hands tangled in hair, deep breathless kisses, their legs entwined, their hard cocks rubbing against one another.

"This has always been my favorite room," said the ghost with a chuckle as he turned Jonas onto his stomach. He nestled himself against Jonas's backside and wrapped his arm around Jonas's torso, kissing his shoulders and the nape of his neck. He nipped at Jonas's earlobe and said huskily, "I hope you enjoy being my guest here."

And then he was inside Jonas. Filling him completely, driving away the emptiness.

There was nothing ghostly, and certainly everything corporeal about what was happening now. His eyes fluttered shut, and Jonas threw back his head, moaning. He clutched at the bedsheets, balling them into knots in his hands. He felt the need to secure himself to the earth, as though he were being lifted on a cloud of fog and carried up and above the trees and nearer and nearer to the warming glow of the sun. The darkness itself became a flooding of light, and he opened his mouth to cry out as the clouds released their gathering pressure and the fresh storm within him broke.

Chapter Eight

The next morning Jonas woke to the sunlight streaming through the open windows. He was tangled in the bedclothes, which had been practically torn from the mattress, and still naked underneath. A moment of shame flashed over him as he heard a noise near the fire. Poor Sarah, he thought, what must she have thought, coming onto this sight at daybreak? But, of course, she had likely seen much more scandalous in her time in this house. The thought almost made him giddy with laughter and he stifled a chuckle. Perhaps he was indeed going insane. After the jagged cliffs and perilous valleys of emotions he had experienced the night before, he wasn't entirely sure he could be of sound mind. Had he really made love to a ghost? How indeed was that possible?

But, of course, it wasn't. Still, he could not explain how the man from the painting had been there alive, very much in the warm and living flesh, in his bedroom. He had felt the spirit inside him—he must have—but how? The oddest part of the realization was how astonishingly alive he felt now—as if some part of him forgotten had been awakened. Either he was indeed mad, or this terrible stone heap had cast some sort of spell over him. He wasn't sure he could stand to find out which was true. As soon as he had finished breakfast and made his apologies to the ladies, he would rouse Donaldson and make his way back to London. When Lord Stanley returned—if, in fact, he ever did—he might come back and entertain their query. But, for now, he felt it best to get away from the torrent of emotions in which he had been drowning over the last two days.

Last night had awakened in him a need so great, so acute, for love, for affection, that he doubted he could concentrate on work. All he could think of now was the thrill his night—his fevered dream possibly? —with the ghost had given him. It was like the perilous heights of ecstasy he had once felt with Marcus. Only another man—another loving body—close to him could demand his attention in this frame of mind. He need something real, something he could claim, not the promise of something bodiless, a metaphysical lover, no matter the level of physical joy it brought him.

He had to sort himself out.

He cleared his throat.

"I say, good morning, Sarah."

"Morning, sir."

"Have I overslept again?"

"Not at all, sir. The family is just rising for breakfast themselves. Should be down shortly."

"Splendid. I am ravenous," he admitted.

"Her ladyship asked for a full spread this morning, of course. Extras of—"

Sarah broke off as the service panel clicked open. They both turned to see Cecil emerge. Sarah quickly began to gather her things, a scornful expression on her face.

"Good morning, sir," she said as she attempted to slide past Cecil and into the corridor.

"Hello, my little biscuit," Cecil said, his tone teasing. He moved back and forth, blocking her exit.

Her hands full, Sarah shoved at him with an elbow.

"Bugger off, Cecil, you clod." She glanced at Jonas. "Begging your pardon, sir."

"Not at all, Sarah. Do let the girl pass, Cecil."

Cecil stepped to the side to allow her by, bending down to growl when she came close. She elbowed him as hard as she could and trotted off down the passageway. Cecil pushed the panel shut and leaned against it chuckling.

"What an empty-headed sausage, that one."

"I find her rather endearing," countered Jonas, not at all in the mood for Cecil's shenanigans.

Cecil shook his head and moved forward, bending to retrieve something from the floor. It was Jonas's crumpled and dirty nightshirt. Cecil looked at it, smirking, as he moved around to the foot of the bed. He tossed the nightshirt at Jonas.

"My goodness, sir, what devilment did you get up to after I left you last night?"

Jonas got out of bed, snatched the long shirt from Cecil's hands, and pulled it on.

"I can only imagine what Sarah must have thought," said Jonas.

"I don't expect she minded much," said Cecil, going to the fire. He picked up the mud-encrusted shoes there. He raised his brows.

"I had to go outside briefly," Jonas said.

Cecil bent to return the shoes to the floor. "More of those bad dreams, I expect."

"Bad dreams?" Jonas froze. "What do you know of my dreams?"

"Only about those you had your first night here when you imagined you had been seduced by a spirit who snuck into the room and magically pinned you to the bed as he sucked your cock." Cecil scoffed and leered at him. "You have quite the imagination, sir, I must admit. I have been complimented on my abilities but never told I sent spasms of electricity through a body."

Jonas felt all of the air knocked out of him. He was speechless.

Cecil leaned back against the mantle and stared at him.

"What did you put in the tea?" Jonas managed to ask.

"Oh, that. That were just a little tincture of herbs. Her ladyship has quite the herb garden, as you know. They usually mix that one special, almost as good as laudanum, they say. For toothache and that. Just a little dab usually. It's a good job you didn't drink the whole cup, I reckon. Next time I'll know better how much to use."

Jonas shook his head, stunned. "You drugged me, for what purpose? I would have been willing. What indecent thrill could you get from imprisoning a

man's body between half-sleeping and half-wak-
ing?"

Cecil gave him an admonishing look. "Indecent?"
He tutted. "Hardly, sir. And, I must say, your body
seemed to respond quite easily. I'd hardly call that a
prison."

"You disgust me."

"Come now, sir. Only you do seem to like the dra-
matics, don't you? I thought it would be something
just your cup of tea if you'll pardon the expression."

Cecil chuckled at his own joke, and Jonas turned
away, trying to compose himself. He wanted to cut
him with words, but he found he had none for this
creature.

Cecil's eyes narrowed, there was more still he
wanted to say.

"After all, sir, I reckon that was quite the scene of
playacting you put on in the chapel last night," Cecil
said, his voice sour. "What dreams that must have
inspired afterwards."

Jonas spun around. "The chapel? That was you?"

Cecil broke into laughter. "Oh, sir, you should
have seen your face!"

He twisted his features into a mask of fright.

"M-M-Marcus, is th-th-that you?" he cried out.

"Why you bastard," Jonas clenched his fist at his
side in anger.

"You'll have to forgive me, sir. But when I saw
you fly down those stairs in nothing but your nightshirt and shoes, I had to pull one on you. It was far
too easy. You seemed particularly outdone by that
ghastly old painting. Cursing at it like it were a real

man. Is that what set you off so? And then after you took your little tumble down the hill, I managed to sneak into the chapel to watch you hidden. Lucky me the rain drove you in. What were you looking for in the garden anyway?"

"You are despicable."

"Oh, come now, sir. It were only a little joking. Don't be so sour." A cold edge came into his voice then, and any expression of amusement left it. "We have to take our entertainment where we can, didn't you say."

Jonas gnashed his teeth. How dare he try to use his words against him? He had done nothing to ask for this sort of treatment.

"Those things you called out in the chapel, those names; that was more than a joke. How did you know those things?" Jonas asked, although on some level he already knew the answer.

"Well, sir, you can't leave your diary lying around and not expect eyes to see it, can you?"

Jonas rushed at him, grabbing his by the jacket and swinging him around the foot of the bed. He was pushing him towards the service panel. He wanted him out.

Cecil grabbed his forearms.

"There we go, Jonas," he said. "That's what I could sense underneath. That's what I wanted. You might dress the part well enough, but you're no gentleman, are you? Sir!"

He spat the last word with venom.

"Under all them pretty clothes and that posh voice, we're not so different, are we, Mister Laurence?"

"I may not be a gentleman, but I am nothing like you. What joy could it bring you to mistreat someone, a virtual stranger, in such a way? To tear into their heart and dredge up memories and hurt. Is it purely for your own amusement?"

Cecil answered with a jeering laugh.

"What do you know of my life?" Cecil growled. "You can't know the things I've put up with, the treachery that's been done upon me."

"No, I can't know. But it's pitiable that it has brought you so low. That it has made you nothing more than a black-hearted trickster."

"Well, you certainly didn't mind my black heart or my body as a substitute for your poor precious Marcus did you?"

Jonas saw red then and before he knew it he had struck the man.

Cecil stumbled backward, rubbing his jaw.

"You fucking bastard," Cecil hissed.

"Get out!" roared Jonas. "Get out of my room! Out of my sight!"

He shoved Cecil back against the service panel, popping it open. Jonas snatched it wide and grabbed Cecil by the shoulder.

"Get your hands off me," Cecil shouted, and pushed Jonas. He grabbed the panel door and angled himself behind it. "You'll regret this, you stupid gardener. You can't treat me like this; I'll make you pay up!"

"The only thing I regret is ever having touched you," Jonas said through gritted teeth.

And with that he leveled the panel with a kick, throwing Cecil back into the passage. Jonas pushed it shut and leaned against it.

He tried to calm his breathing, to still his anger. What a fool he had been. Allowing himself to be manipulated for deranged thrills by that sinister cretin. And for what? Mere pleasures of the body. Cecil was right about one thing, he had been stupid. Stupid and reckless.

Stumbling over to the water pitcher, he poured some into the washing bowl. He gasped at the icy temperature, but, despite its chill, he ripped off his nightshirt and began splashing the water all over his face and neck and chest until he was shivering. He grabbed the flannel from beside the basin and dried himself off.

He flopped down into the chair of the writing desk, pressing the flannel onto his face. He dropped it in his lap and pulled his diary towards him. The watercolor sketches came with it. He ran his finger along the edge of a particularly sunny-looking sketch, all bright greens and yellows and reds. How could such a house be both so creepy and have the promise of such sunshine and light?

For a moment, Jonas regretted his decision to flee back to London. Was this only his second morning in this house? It seemed hard to fathom. The people and the atmosphere had been at such juxtaposition, it was hard to reconcile them. And, in some strange way, the events of the last twelve hours or so had been a significant catharsis. He had been forced to face head-on so many unresolved feelings, and in the strangest of ways, he felt more whole now despite having been shaken quite loose.

But, above all, he could not remain here, naked at his writing-table, waiting to shock whatever poor maid might wander in next. He must get downstairs and express his feelings to Vita.

As he entered the dining room, Vita was there reading her paper over a plate of kedgeree and deviled kidneys.

"Ah, good morning, Jonas."

"Lady Stanley. Good morning."

She gave him a searching look. "Are we as formal as all that again?"

"I am afraid there's something I must discuss."

"Surely not on an empty stomach, no matter how dire. Please have some breakfast."

He considered it a moment, his stomach rumbling, but best to deliver the news before he changed his mind. He sat down. "I'm afraid I have to make my apologies, Lady Stanley, but I must return to London."

She quickly closed her paper and put it down.

"Is there some emergency?"

Jonas shook his head. "Not as you would say. Something more akin to an emergency of conscience."

"Oh no, please don't say that, Jonas. We had hoped you would stay for a few days at least. It would be such a shame for you to leave now, and with Graham only just back."

"His lordship is back? But I thought he had been delayed again."

She lifted her brows. "So his telegram suggested, but he managed to disentangle himself somehow and returned very late yesterday evening," she said, her tone wry. "Sometime after dinner, near the middle of the night, he arrived. I'm surprised you weren't disturbed, there was ever such a commotion."

"I had fallen deeply asleep," he said, wary of revealing his nighttime activities. "With a book in bed, quite tired."

"Of course. I'm glad you weren't distracted. It was quite something and then those bloody hounds howling all over the place."

A shiver went through Jonas. "Hounds?"

"Oh yes, he took the dogs with him to London—he usually does, though I can't imagine why. And they were positively shot through with restlessness when he finally set them free of the car. He had them running the grounds for what seemed like hours. Luckily dear Christopher could sleep through a typhoon."

"Dogs, running the grounds," he muttered.

"Yes, until it began to rain again. Then he brought them in."

"Yes, I did hear the barking as a matter of fact. I had forgotten."

"I thought you must have, it was positively deafening. I trust you weren't too disturbed?"

"No, not at all, I just noticed them but thought nothing more."

"I thought, in fact, you might run into Graham this morning in the East Hall. Oh, but here he is now." Her gaze traveled behind Jonas. "I'm sure he can convince you to give us another chance."

Jonas began to rise and turn towards the doorway. What he saw made him fall back into his seat with a thud.

"Oh, dear," said Vita.

"My dear fellow," said Lord Stanley. "Are you quite all right?"

All right? Jonas wanted to shout. *No, of course, I am not all right. You are a ghost! You are the man from the painting come to life! The phantom waiting for me in my room last night—the creature that has haunted my dreams for two days. The ghost who seduced me!* And, realizing how ridiculous it all seemed, he felt as if he had been repeatedly slapped across the face.

"But... only...it's just...the painting," he managed to stutter.

"Ah, yes," said Graham with a guffaw. "That damned painting."

"Yes, isn't the resemblance too, too terrible?" asked Vita. "As I told you, I often tease him about it."

"But, of course," said Graham, moving into the room, "most people meet me before the painting so the resemblance is usually seen the other way round."

"We ought to remove that horrid thing," said Vita. "I often feel as if it watches me as I walk."

"Do you mind so very much a face just like your husband's watching you?" Graham teased. "Besides, Mamma would never hear of it."

"If she wants electricity in her bedroom, she just might," Vita said archly.

Jonas found his voice. "Lord Stanley, I'm afraid there is something I must discuss with you."

"Please call me Graham. And yes, of course, we'll take a stroll of the grounds after we eat."

Jonas cleared his throat and inhaled deeply.

"No," he declared. "I think now, Lord Stanley."

Vita looked surprised and her husband bemused.

"Why, yes, Mister Laurence, if you insist."

"I do."

Jonas stalked outside and waited for Lord Stanley to follow. When he emerged, Jonas waved him on.

"Please," he said, "a little farther from the house."

"But, Mister—"

"So that we are not overheard, thank you."

They reached the end of the *porte-cochère* and Jonas spun around, no longer able to control his feelings.

He came up close to Lord Stanley and thumped him on the chest, leaving the gentleman bewildered.

"Do tell me, please, what the hell was the meaning of last night?" his voice a barely controlled bellow.

Graham shook his head, in utter confusion.

"But, my dear man, I thought you were open to the idea. I got the telegram from Vita in the morning that things seemed to be going swimmingly. It's why I decided to hasten my return. I was under the impression that she thought we would make a good fit. So I was quite eager to meet you, and when I saw you there in the window, and you invited me up, I just assumed—"

"Invited you up?" exclaimed Jonas.

"Yes, you lifted your hand and then nodded. I merely assumed I was welcome. I admit I am not usually quite so forward in my attentions, nor so… aggressive as that. But when I came to you, I was quite taken—"

"And, just a moment," said Jonas, his thoughts tumbling over themselves. "You say your wife sent you a telegram about me?"

Graham gave a small grimace, and for the first time did not look confused. "Well, yes, I'm sorry, chap. Was that indecent of us? It's just that I knew of you by reputation, of course, and the way Derrick talked of you, he seemed to think we would be a good match as well."

"Derrick? A match?" Jonas's mind was spinning. "But all this business of— I feel quite had—this damned pretense of a ghost…. None of it makes sense. After the number your footman ran on me, I am suspicious of everything in this house, I must confess plainly."

Graham stepped forward and put his hand on Jonas's shoulder.

"Footman?" he asked, his voice concerned. "What do you mean?"

"That young man, Cecil, who was valeting for me. He is quite a devious creature, you know."

"Oh good lord," exclaimed Graham. "Yes, I do indeed know. I implored Vita to sack him long ago. He has been all manner of trouble since we hired him. Filling the maids' heads with tall tales and playing jokes on our guests. As I see he must have done with you."

Jonas let out a large exhalation of breath. "In a way, yes."

"He can be charming when he needs to be. Very charming. Which only succeeds in making the blade of the knife even sharper when he drives it in. Believe me, I have experienced his prick before." He squared his shoulders. "My apologies only. Not to worry, I shall handle Cecil immediately. It was time he found a new position in a new house. I won't tolerate this kind of behavior. And I certainly don't want him driving someone like you away."

Jonas blinked and began to breathe more normally.

"I know it was only hours ago," continued Graham. "But I rather felt like last night was, well, something special and unusual. It was rough and ready, I know. And for that, I apologize. This is my home, a comfortable home, and not some back alley in Ipswich. It's not at all how I intended for our meeting to proceed. I thought we would have more time to become so close. That was my plan at least."

"Your 'plan'?" asked Jonas. "I feel as if I have been slotted into some bizarre puzzle which I never knew existed. I really don't know what to make of all the machinations which surround me."

"I know we only knew each other very little before last night, but I thought possibly if you accepted the offer to come visit then it meant—"

Jonas held up his hand. "My apologies, Lord Stanley, but though you seem to know an awful lot about me, I cannot say the same."

Graham looked at him, with a new expression.

"Good lord," he said, his voice low. "I was a fool to think you might remember."

"Remember?" asked Jonas.

"Would you walk with me, please?" asked Graham tenderly.

They walked, without speaking, until they came to a bench in the back garden. Graham held out his hand for Jonas to sit, which he did, rather gratefully as exhaustion seemed to threaten every fiber of his being. Graham sat beside him and they both gazed out over the grounds for a moment before he spoke.

"The first time we met was about two years ago, at one of those stupid club functions where all the chaps in London sit around with the cigars and business cards and pretend to be doing something, anything, worthwhile. We didn't say much more than hello, and you were surrounded most of the evening by associates, chatting at you. But I couldn't take my eyes off of you. All night, talking or drinking or pretending to listen to some boring old coot, I was watching you. I wanted so badly to speak with you, but I could not muster the courage. And, of course, there is that worry, isn't there? You never know if a chap is similarly inclined and the fear of giving one's self away and causing an irreparable scene is daunting."

"Yes, of course," said Jonas quietly.

Something fluttered in the back of Jonas's mind, a vague memory. Of course, how could he have been so obtuse? He now realized why the face in the painting felt so familiar, so haunting. It had felt like some deep-seated memory that he couldn't quite bring into focus. And, now, he realized that was exactly what it was. He did not remember meeting Graham before, but that handsome face had stuck with him, somewhere in the recesses of his mind. How could one forget such a face, after all? Knowing his emotional habits, he might very well have been struck by Graham's beauty but buried the distraction deep in an attempt to devote his attention fully to his relationship with Pearson. He had been trying so very hard for so very long to be what he assumed others needed him to be.

"But just before you left the club that night," continued Graham, "I saw you speaking with Derrick. You seemed rather familiar, and so after you left, I pulled my cousin aside and inquired as to who you were. Of course, he confirmed that you were the long spoken of partner, Jonas Laurence, and I was buoyed. I cheered immediately knowing that here must be my in. I suppose it read on my face, and my cousin is not quite as stupid as he often pretends to be, so he casually let me know that you and your associate, a chap named Pearson, I believe?"

Jonas could only nod.

"That the two of you had quite a comfortable situation in the city. My hopes were dashed, but not the flame that had been lit when seeing you. I thought myself rather casual, but I'm sure Derrick was not oblivious to my sudden interest in his firm and his partners, particularly you. Whenever we spoke, he kept me abreast of how things were progressing and I longed for the chance to see you again."

He turned to Jonas. His study was not intense or threatening, but rather soft and tender. Something in Jonas told him he ought to be uncomfortable, to recoil from this rabid interest displayed by a virtual stranger, but he was not. Instead, he was touched, moved somewhere, and in some way he could not identify. When he looked into Graham's eyes, his mind was flooded with memories of the feeling of Graham's arms around him, Graham's kisses against his skin, Graham inside him. He wanted those feelings again; he yearned for them. Yearned for them so deeply that he thought he might crack into two from the force of his emotions.

"I got my chance," continued Graham. "It was just a little less than a year ago. The party at Derrick's townhouse in the city. It was quite fun and boisterous, as Derrick's parties tend to be. And there you were. Derrick had made a special effort to invite me, I believe; he virtually insisted I must come. At first, I was a bit put out. You arrived with your chap, your Pearson, and I was angry at Derrick. I thought he had brought me there to show me the truth, to put an end to the silly pining I felt. I spoke to you, we were introduced, but you seemed quite distracted. I doubted then that you even registered my presence, or would remember our meeting. And you seem not to have."

Jonas dropped his head, embarrassed. How could he twice have forgotten this man? Had his mind been such a jumble these last two years? He shook his head. He hoped finally that the fog was beginning to clear and the light to stream in; it seemed as if he had been wandering around in some odd fugue state for longer than he realized.

"But I understood, of course," said Graham. "You and your friend seemed very much at odds that evening, and you, especially, looked rather miserable. I tried to conduct myself properly, to enjoy the party as I ought. But, of course, I kept watch over you all evening. Then I saw you and Pearson arguing in a corner, quite heatedly, and your friend stormed out. Derrick saw too and he encouraged me to swoop in, to play some sort of rescuer. To take advantage of the situation. But I couldn't do it. It wasn't right, not then, not in the middle of what was clearly an emotional battle for you. You looked wounded, and my heart was sick for you."

Graham broke off then and turned away, seeming to search for his next words.

And the memories flooded Jonas.

Jonas remembered the night Graham spoke of well. In fact, perhaps too well, indeed. It had been the night that he knew it was over. Pearson and

Jonas had been having rows for weeks previous, petty arguments, sometimes full-on shouting matches. Pearson had come to the end of his emotional tether; he had accused Jonas of never being around, of using the social need for the pretense of "just friendship" as an excuse in order to keep him distant, to shut him out. Jonas denied these accusations then, even as he knew, on some level, that they were true. He hadn't meant to shut Pearson out, he had loved him, once, or so he thought, but that gnawing ache of emptiness would not let him be. That feeling that there was something, someone maybe, missing from his life.

He had pleaded with Pearson to give him another chance and their tension had quieted for a bit. But on the night of the party at Derrick's, things had taken a turn. Jonas had been icy, even snappish and rude, and had done his best to keep everyone at arm's length, especially Pearson. It was a good thing, in retrospect, that Graham had not tried to speak to him that night. He would have likely left a sour taste in the mouth, given his state.

Jonas leaned back on the bench and ran his hands over his face, ashamed of the feelings his memories dredged up.

What he had not been able to tell Pearson then, and what he had never told anyone, was that he had received a letter the day before. Another letter from Marcus's sister, or, rather, this time about Marcus's sister. He had received a letter saying that she had passed away, struck down with pneumonia. Although she and Jonas had never been close friends, she had kept in touch with him throughout the years. They had exchanged letters and, on rare occasions, shared lunch in the city. But past their casual friendship, and most importantly, she had been his only remaining tie to Marcus. He had not realized, until he received the news of her death, how much he had cherished that tie, how much he needed it. It was the one thing he had left of Marcus, and somehow it gave him some sense of still being attached to that depth of love he had once felt. With her gone, the tie was severed, and a storm of emotion had broken loose within him that he did not have the power to control. Everyone became his enemy, it seemed, especially those who loved him most, who expected to be loved back.

Like Pearson.

Pearson had gone on an unexpected trip, to the Mediterranean, with some friends mere days after the party. When he returned, both he and Jonas had vowed to give it one more try. And although they had stumbled through the winter months, in a shabby sham of what they once had, it was not the same. They both knew it. Only Pearson had been the one brave enough to finally call it done. To finally turn Jonas loose from shackles of guilt that had kept them bound together.

He had wanted to be so much more for Pearson, to be all he knew the man deserved, but he had not had it in him. Until the spectre of Marcus had vanished from his life, he had never let himself be whole. Now he knew this to be true, though it had taken him all these months to realize. Now, he knew, he might finally be a complete man now, ready and willing to love.

Graham cleared his throat, and rubbed the palms of his hands along his thighs.

"Last night," Graham said, "when I came to you in your room, there was something in your manor, your mood, which reminded me of that night at Derrick's party. But now, instead of trying to hide that hurt so obviously roiling inside, you seemed so open, so raw, so in need of tenderness, and it struck something in me terribly. A depth of passion I haven't felt in some time, even surpassing what I thought I already felt for you. I had a picture of you in my mind all this time, a picture of what I thought you were, and what we might be, but I never thought it could be real. Until last night. Finding you like that, having you like that, it made me know that it was not just an imagining."

He looked deep into Jonas's eyes. "Moments like that present themselves so rarely in life. Once, maybe twice, if we're lucky. It seems against nature to turn away from it. I would hate to live with the regret of not at least trying to see if there was something more there," said Graham. "Wouldn't you?"

Something like a sob caught at the back of Jonas's throat and he found it hard to speak. He wanted to yell it out, say yes, yes, yes until his throat was raw. But caution only allowed him so much.

"Yes," he said quietly. "I would."

They sat for a moment without speaking. Jonas stared across the landscape. The lake, which had seemed so far away before, was bright in the day's sunlight. Shimmering and blue, it seemed to be filled with light as its ripples lapped against the shore.

"All of this then," he finally said, "the garden, the job, was all a ruse? Just to get us to meet again?"

"Not at all," Graham said. "But I thought it was worth a try. When I contacted Derrick a couple of months ago with my interest in doing something with it, he casually let slip that you might be free. That you and Pearson were going your separate ways, and that the work would do you a good distraction. If you had no interest in me but you did in our gardens then I would get a splendid new grounds if nothing else. But, of course, I cannot lie and say I didn't hope for me."

"Good," said Jonas. "Because there is something that touches me about this place. When I first arrived, I must be honest, something about it disturbed me. But, even then, I found it quite beautiful." His mind went back to his earlier thought of catharsis. "Now, just this morning, on this new day, something calls me. I feel as if, in some queer way, I belong to this place. Your wife said something similar before, but I thought she was only flattering. Now I look out and see that I have come to a resting spot. All my other work, for so many years, has been this burst of energy and expulsion of noise from my mind. I like to think that I occasionally created something beautiful. But, I never lingered, I never let myself be settled. I have been running, from project to project, for a very long time. Here, I feel as if I might stop for a moment. I might finally listen to what the landscape is telling me, what it is whispering to me when I am quiet, instead of screaming my voice until it submits to my design, my plans. Because I have learned plans seldom mean much in the end."

Graham was looking at him, a bewitching smile on his face.

"That is the voice I saw in your articles," he said. "That is the artist I heard in your words."

Jonas was surprised. "You read my articles? I didn't know that anyone ever laid eyes on them."

Graham laughed. "I suppose I sound like an infatuated schoolgirl. But, yes. Derrick sent me a copy of *The Country Estate* when you first published there years ago. He was quite proud, you know; don't let his vinegar tongue fool you. The essay moved me, and I insisted on getting my own subscription after that. Reading your writing was part of what fed my desire to first meet you. I heard your voice on the page, and it sparked my dreams."

"How was I to predict you'd be so damned irresistibly handsome as well?"

Jonas ducked his head, trying to hide his smile.

Graham let his pinky run along the side of Jonas's hand on the bench. "Is it only the gardens then which compel your interest?" he asked softly.

Jonas met his gaze. "No. Not only. There is something that touches me deeply about you as well. Somehow I don't feel as if I should be running any longer. Perhaps it makes no sense, us knowing each other so briefly. But there it is."

"Things needn't always make sense to be true," said Graham.

He leaned in and kissed Jonas sweetly, tenderly. Jonas shut his eyes tightly as they kissed, something in him wanting it never to end.

"Do you think," asked Graham, "that we might make a new start of it? Wipe the slate clean, as it were, and see if we might explore something together?"

Jonas nodded. "I would like that very much indeed. But what of Vita?"

Graham smiled broadly, his voice was bright. "Dear, amazing Vita. My dear man, don't you know she is quite content and knows all? Vita has known me like no other person has known me, ever since we were children. In fact, we rather share the same taste in men." He winked at Jonas then and laughed brightly. "This whole arrangement—our marriage, I mean—was, in fact, her idea. There have been no secrets or illusions between us. Vita was not meant to be someone's "proper" wife, trotted out for formal occasions, and composing seating charts. She would go insane with boredom if her life were nothing more than a mere companion or ornament to a man, But she, just like I, enjoys and appreciates a comfortable life. So here we are. We share a child whom we both adore, and we both live a life full of our own interests and pursuits."

"I have rather felt as if I were being summed up these last few days," conceded Jonas.

"My wonderful wife has innumerable delightful qualities, but subtlety is not among them." Graham stood from the bench and offered his hand to Jonas. "Shall we make a start of the day, then, and see where it takes us?"

"Yes, let's."

As they reached the front of the house, Jonas remembered the start of the morning's agitation.

"I must admit one detail that I may have left out before," he began.

"Yes? What is that?" asked Graham.

Jonas cleared his throat. "Yes, well, as pertains to Cecil."

"The bastard footman; yes, go on."

"Yes, well, you see, Graham. This morning, in a fit of agitation, I may have struck him."

Lord Stanley's mouth fell open. "Cecil? You struck Cecil?"

"I'm afraid so. I punched him—in the jaw. In my defense—"

But he was interrupted by the other man's laughter. Graham was practically bent in half by the force of his amusement. His laughter rang out.

"Oh, my good man," he said, wiping the tears from his eyes. "I cannot explain the depth of affection I feel for you in this moment. If you struck that rotten fool, I can assure it was overdue and deserved, and I applaud you for it."

He clapped Jonas on the shoulder and the relief sent Jonas into a fit of laughter himself. It was just the release he needed after his morning of agitation and worry, and the laughter rolled on and on growing louder and fuller. This set Graham to laughing again as well and it was this scene of nearly crazed merriment upon which the Dowager Countess and Lady Aldrange came.

The two ladies, holding hands, walked up to them and both smiled.

"Just as we suspected," said the dowager. "The two of you have got on together immediately. You know, I had a feeling this might happen. I told Vita so the moment I met you, Mister Laurence."

"She did," agreed Lady Aldrange. "And, Mister Laurence, do you know we have just been to see that marvelous chauffeur of yours again."

"Donaldson?"

"The very one. We went out early before breakfast to catch him before he began any of his mechanics and that sort of thing. We so enjoyed our ride yesterday into the village, and we had so many questions for him. It was rather illuminating, and we must confess, we have decided to purchase an automobile ourselves."

"And I plan to learn to drive," declared the Dowager Countess.

"Mamma?" Graham was surprised.

"I do!" she continued. "Do you know, Donaldson says that many women drive? There are even books to the effect, special manuals for lady drivers. As well as gloves, face goggles, and an entire wardrobe especially for it."

"You know," said Graham. "I can just see it now."

"Yes," agreed Jonas. "I think it would be top-notch."

"Mister Laurence," said Lady Aldrange. "I sincerely hope you don't mind my saying, but you look rather exhausted."

He sighed audibly. "Yes, your ladyship, I am rather. More than you might imagine. It was somewhat of a long night."

"Then after breakfast, you must allow me to arrange for some of my salts and herbals for your bathing. Graham has quite a large tub in his room, just next to yours. I'm sure he wouldn't mind giving you the use of it for a good long soak. It will be just the thing to soothe away any troubles."

"What do you say," said Graham. "To a good long relax in my room, Mister Laurence? Surely you don't need to run off to London, after all."

"Oh, were you planning to leave, Mister Laurence? I do hope not," said the Dowager Countess.

"He did mention to Vita that he might have to," said Graham. He glanced at Jonas. "But, Mamma, I am hoping our talk just now has convinced him to stay here for quite a bit longer."

Jonas smiled sheepishly and tried not to seem too coy when he replied, "Yes, I think I could be persuaded, after all."

"Splendid," said the Dowager Countess. "I do so enjoy when all the pieces fall into place."

"Ladies, shall we breakfast?" asked Lord Stanley as he extended his arm to his mother. She took it with a smile and Jonas offered the same to Lady Aldrange.

"Oh, look, there's Vita," said Lady Aldrange.

"Hello, darling," said Graham. "Have you finished breakfast already?"

"Yes, dearest, I have," said Vita. "I'm off to the stables for my morning ride."

"Great day for it," he said. "Give Patrick my apologies, won't you? I'm afraid my arrival last night rather jolted him a bit. I know he doesn't at all care for my hounds. I hope I didn't upset him too much."

"I'm sure he can be soothed," she said. "And Mister Laurence." Vita stopped by him and put her hand on his free arm. "Has my husband convinced you to stay on? Do say yes."

"Jonas, please. And, yes, he has convinced me. I am actually looking quite forward to our collaboration."

Vita pressed her hand to his cheek. He was surprised at the warmth he felt.

"There, you see," said Vita, with a bright smile, "I knew it would be a marvelous match."

She leaned in and kissed him on the cheek and smiled at her mamma before she was off again towards the stables.

"She does so love her riding, my daughter," said Lady Aldrange, patting his arm. "And have you noticed, Mister Laurence? The rain has disappeared entirely. The sun is out and shining, everything bright and green. What a lovely picture of a day—perfect for getting lost in the gardens."

Graham turned back to them and smiled, winking at Jonas.

"Yes," said Jonas, quite in agreement, "it is a lovely picture indeed."

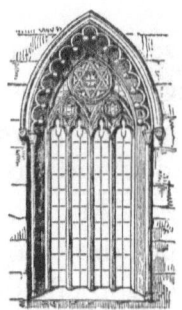

Chapter Nine

The Harvest Moon

England, 1834

With the jovial noises of chatter and song behind him, Malcolm came out of the public house and into the crisp night. He had taken drink tonight, not overly much, but even so, he needed fresh air. The patrons were nice enough but he  was somehow, despite the darkness of the hour, compelled to be outside. He yearned to feel a breeze against his skin, to gaze at the moon, to be amongst nature itself. Nearby the tavern was a small clearing lit by the night sky, and he made his way to it.

He was still surprised to find himself in this village, which he had never noticed before in all the years he had been traveling back and forth from his estate to that of his great aunt. On its surface, it was an ordinary little village, with not very much at all to distinguish it. Nothing of note had attracted him when first encountered earlier the same day, and save the fact that his poor horse, Grannus, had been exhausted from a rainy day of trudging through mud, he might not have stopped.

As he and Grannus had entered the village, he'd been taken by the remarkable copse of trees which seemed to mark the entrance into the main part of the little hamlet. The trees grew in such a fashion, almost like columns turning in a design, as to suggest an archway. Like the start of some old, great Roman road, cutting through the brambles and hedgerows.

With the help of a few locals, peering from the front doors of their cottages at the unexpected visitor, he soon discovered what was deemed the best inn available, and from what he could tell the only inn available. He was happy to discover that it was a tidy and cozy tavern, mainly operating as a public house with a few small but well-kept rooms on top. Bone weary as he was, he would have taken a bale of hay, so a proper bed was all the more warmly received.

He was growing old, he suspected. At twenty and eight, and the last male heir of his line, he was frequently lambasted by his great aunt for having not yet found a wife. He had no interest in a wife, or in women for that matter, but of course, that was not a thing one could share. He knew his great aunt considered it his sole obligation, but his concerns for his future legacy only ran to his sisters. He had built a large fortune and his investments were vast, and he meant for his two sisters to be well-provided for, whether they chose to marry or not. Past that, he had no thoughts of fulfilling any duty assumed of him.

Standing there in the small clearing, he had a thought that the sway of the trees sounded almost like a chorus of whispers. It was a silly, childish thought and he laughed to himself. A movement in the nearby brush caught his attention. He heard rustling within the trees but could not make out its source. He felt no apprehension, but he knew, even in a place as simple as this village, one still needed to keep one's guard. He called out.

"Is somebody there?"

A shadow, a crouched lurking figure, moved behind a tree. His hand went to his belt for the pistol he usually carried there. It was absent, having been left in his room when he'd changed out of his wet garments. He silently cursed his dereliction.

"I say, have you any business here?" Malcolm said loudly, taking a step forward.

"No sir," came a husky male voice. "Only observing."

"Why observing? There's good humor and ale to go around. I can't think you wouldn't be welcome."

"I shouldn't be, sir." The voice replied. The figure moved from behind the tree and stepped in the circle of moonlight that fell nearby. "It wouldn't be right."

The moonlight revealed the voice to belong to a young man, perhaps Malcolm's junior by only two or three years.

And what a magnificent young man he was. His face was of a beauty and freshness such that Malcolm had hardly ever seen. Even here in the darkness of night, standing in the cast of moon glow, he appeared to have cheeks touched by the rosy bloom of health. He was lean but not at all gaunt in the way many country laborers were. He was tall and wore no hat, his face framed by wavy titian hair that curled at its edges. Simple in design but expertly made, his clothing fell on his frame just as it should. They were plain country garments but a master hand had turned the loom and cut the cloth. His broad shoulders and slim waist repaid the craftsmanship by being perfectly proportioned.

Without thinking, Malcolm had begun to approach the young man slowly. He felt compelled by a force as if a rope had been tied around his waist and pulled him steadily forward. He stepped into the circle of moonlight and realized that he had been staring openly in stupid silence, and halted.

Embarrassed, he opened his mouth to say something, anything, and the stranger dipped his head, smiling bashfully. That small gesture inflamed Malcolm's passion and he instantly forgot his discomfiture. The two exchanged smiles.

"What is your name?" Malcolm asked.

"Daniel," he answered. "Daniel Weaver they call me, as my family have always been of the trade."

"Did your family make these clothes?"

"Yes, sir. By my own hand," Daniel said, proudly.

"Won't you sit with me and take a drink?" asked Malcolm, gesturing towards the tavern.

"As I said, sir, it would not be good."

"Your wife waiting at home?" asked Malcolm.

"I have no wife."

"Your betrothed, then?"

"Sir, I think you will find that I am quite unattached in that manner."

"As am I."

"Yes, I thought so."

"So quickly surmised?" A hint of embarrassment crept back as Malcolm thought of his immediate reaction to the sight of Daniel.

"You paid no heed to any of the wenches inside," said Daniel. "And kept mainly to yourself, or the company of a friendly gentleman or two."

"Have you been watching me all evening?" asked Malcolm, surprised. "I didn't see you inside."

"No, I watched from outside. Through the open door. I have noticed you since you arrived this midday."

Daniel stepped towards him and Malcolm, slightly astonished, felt his nature rise. Still, he was wary.

"I thought you were a weaver, sir. Not a huntsman."

"Surely a man can have many skills?" Daniel raised a brow and smiled coyly.

"You are bold, sir," Malcolm said with a half-smile. "And yet you hover in the shadows instead of joining the conviviality."

Daniel shrugged, his jaw set. "My fellow villagers are not as welcoming to me as they are to you," he said. "I have never been part of their flock."

Malcolm knew that feeling well, it was a battle he had fought his whole life. Struggling to present a version of himself that everyone found acceptable, even if it was wholly bland without and spiritually stultifying within.

"I understand," he said.

"I thought you might." Daniel studied his face for a moment. "I wonder, sir, if you might partake of my hospitality."

"Hospitality?"

"Though I choose not to mingle with the flock, my own home is well supplied with a jug of ale and a warm hearth." His eyes met Malcolm's and they seemed to shimmer in the moon's glow. "Could I beseech you to join me there?"

Malcolm's breath caught and he blinked, his head feeling light. Possibly too much drink already, he thought, but surely a nice fire and the... company of this young man would be just the thing. It had been a long while since he shared in the companionship of his fellow man, and the need, he admitted, was strong within him.

"With pleasure, sir."

The woods, as they made their way, were very still and quiet. He did not sense the scurry of any small animals nor hear the flutter of birds that usually populated the night forest. It seemed to him that he was making a lot of noise, brush cracking underfoot. Every step made him slightly self-conscious as if at any moment someone might spring from the branches and overtake them.

Daniel turned and said softly, "Walk here, just behind me."

He moved in behind Daniel and all noise seemingly disappeared. He no longer heard the crepitation of twigs or underbrush. It was odd, to be sure, but presently he forgot its oddness and his nerves settled.

They walked some time without speaking until through the trees Malcolm saw a splintering of light up ahead, like a jewel held up to a candle. He broke off from behind Daniel to follow the glimmer.

He came upon a lake, its surface glittering like a ballroom in season. All around the perimeter, there seemed to be movement. A flock of small birds, of the daytime variety, surprised Malcolm as they flitted and dove around, gliding over the water and then returning to the trees. All manner of insects hummed about as well, their wings catching the light of the moon and reflecting it in tiny shards of iridescence. Across the way, he saw deer, a stag with his mighty antlers, standing majestically at the lake's edge. The trees and shrubbery all around rustled with movement as if every animal of the forest had appeared to worship at the altar of the lake.

Daniel was beside him. They looked out over the scene together.

"It's an astonishing show," said Malcolm. "I have never seen anything like it. It is the dead of night and yet this cove feels as splendid as day."

"It's the moon, of course," said Daniel. "The harvest moon. It is the last full moon before the autumn comes upon us. The night when the warm months are leaving and when nature is welcoming in the darkness and the cold. Everything alive bristles with one last flourish. There, can you see? The moon is said to be at its strongest on these nights. Its power holds the greatest sway just now."

"Power?"

"Yes, power over all the things of nature. They are lured by the pull and glamour of the moon. Some say, old tales of the pagans, that when the moon and the solstice are near in hand like this, it is like a tunnel of sorts that magnifies the echo of nature. That all the things whose force is tied to the land are stronger and more wonderful than usual—they are made fuller. More powerful."

Malcolm looked at Daniel.

"That sounds like magic."

Daniel met his gaze.

"Yes, it does."

Malcolm noticed for the first time how brilliantly green Daniel's eyes were. A deep forest green around the outside of the irises that flowed into the bottomless center of jewel-like clarity. Had his eyes been an instrument then they would have sung from the light that danced in them now. Standing so close, Malcolm could breathe in the scent of him, spicy like cloves or mace, and then the smell of smooth, clean skin, freshly washed. He wanted to kiss Daniel, run his tongue along his lips, and taste him.

"My god," he exclaimed. "You are magnificent."

Daniel dropped his eyes and his cheeks dimpled with a smile. "You flatter me, sir."

"Flattery suggests motive and I simply speak truth. Your beauty moves me." Malcolm chuckled. "I don't know what has come over me. Usually, my tongue is not so free. They must brew a strong drink here."

"Perhaps," agreed Daniel.

"Perhaps." But Malcolm knew that the strange feelings had nothing whatsoever to do with mulled grain. There was something about this boy that caught him, like a spell.

"My cottage is not much farther," Daniel said. "Shall we?"

Malcolm watched the water for a moment longer. It seemed utterly still and then a flutter of ripples announced the breaking of its surface as a wonderfully colored fish popped up from underneath, its mouth open in hunt of the swarming insects, before crashing below the glassy lid and diving out of sight.

He glanced at Daniel. The light reflecting from the lake burnished one side of him, giving him a radiant glow as if he were formed of something glittering and unreal. Malcolm wondered at how such a glorious creature could thrive out here in this forgotten backwater. He would be the toast of any town, the shining firmament of many a ball, and yet here he was, hidden away. It was a shame, thought Malcolm. And yet, at the same time, it seemed as if he belonged to no other place and no other time but this. Here, by this luminous, shimmering tableau of nature; here was his rightful appointment. Like some sort of fairy king.

Their eyes met—Daniel's mesmerizing, sparkling like gemstones. A rush overcame Malcolm's entire body, and he shivered. Sharing that gaze thrilled him more than whole nights spent with some men of memory. If a mere look could inflame his person like this Malcolm wondered what it must be like to feel Daniel's touch, his mouth, his body.

"Shall we?" repeated Daniel, extending his hand.

Malcolm grabbed hold and nodded.

Chapter Ten

I t was a vaguely L-shaped cottage sitting next to a river, nestled among trees that curved at their uppermost part over the cottage like a canopy or arch. Malcolm was struck at how closely they resembled those he had encountered as he'd first entered the village. A series of windows ran along the front of the cottage, just to the side of the doorway. They were mostly crude, glassless openings that were shuttered against the night air. But at the end facing east, there was a set of large mullioned windows, inset by stone, their glass pocketed and wavy and looking ancient. Through these windows, Malcolm saw that another set of similar making took up space on the opposite wall, and between the two he saw a large panel of shimmering color.

"The loom is kept there," said Daniel, noting how he studied. "The windows are set thusly so that they catch as much light as possible for working by."

The fire in the hearth burned bright and warm, unusually so, in fact. Malcolm wondered how it could be going so strong and tidily, left alone for so long.

"Do you live alone?" he asked.

"I live with my grandfather," said Daniel. "Why do you ask?"

"Only the fire."

"Ah, yes. He must have built it up for me before he left. On nights like this, he stays out. Nighttime is what he likes best—you needn't worry about him showing up."

Malcolm took in the sleeping area by the fire—one large bed, covered in a well-made counterpane and two stuffed pillows. Nearest him was the cooking and dining area. He let his hand rest on a thick, crudely carved table that had two matching chairs. In the shelves above there were many books, their spines not easily read, some of which appeared to be ancient, possibly nothing more than collections of hand-scrawled leaves strung together with ribbon. Beside them sat all manner of herbs and dried flowers.

"Are you an herbalist?" he asked.

Daniel smiled. "You see much. It is a skill I learned from my mother, but I am hardly a master."

Taking up the longest length of the cottage was the workspace with all of the weaver's accouterments. At the far end by the windows was the four-poster loom, a length of cloth in progress, strung across its workings. Just behind the threaded heddles, through the glass of the window, Malcolm could see the forest trees swaying. The space between him and the loom was scattered with shuttles, some empty, some already loaded with spun bobbins, bags of cotton which sat beside the grand spinning wheel, its large round reaching towards the ceiling, a thick strand of thread peeking out from its end. And then more shelves, filled with glass jars and clay pots. He could identify a few containing chunks of indigo or the dried husks of madder roots—all used for dyeing. One, in particular, caught his eye and he approached, lifting it from the shelf. Inside the dusty black pearls toppled as he turned the glass jar.

"Cochineal?" he asked.

Daniel leaned against the table and smiled, studying him.

"Indeed," he answered. "You seem to know and notice much about trade. Most men whom I've taken as visitors barely glance at the loom."

Malcolm replaced the jar on the shelf.

"I suppose it has a special place in my heart. My mother was a weaver, you see."

Daniel crossed his arms across his chest, and his mouth opened in surprise.

"Your mother? A weaver?"

"Of a sort. More bobbins and delicate thread than any sort of loom. She did fine work with lace. That's how she met my father. He and his mother visited lacemakers in Nottinghamshire to see about commissioning a wedding dress for his older sister, my aunt. His mother had very specific ideas on how she thought it ought to look. And there he met my mother, who had been working lace since she was naught but knee-high. He fell in love with her and schemed to marry her. His parents didn't approve, naturally, but my parents-to-be wrote letters to each other for nigh on a year before his mother and father relented and allowed him to begin courting. My mother was much below their class, of course, but eventually, they married."

"Why did your grandparents relent?"

"Because of my aunt."

"Of the lace dress?"

Malcolm nodded.

"She was jilted by her fiancée. He absconded on the day before her wedding with her lady's maid. It followed that my aunt fell into such a state of black melancholia that her family never thought she would recover. So I believe my grandmother was only determined to see one of her children married happily and thus weakened in the battle against my mother's social shortcomings."

"And did she recover? Your aunt, I mean."

"Never entirely, no. By the time I knew her she seemed much older than her years and she died still a spinster. Not long before my own mother—she died of the wasting sickness, you see, when I was very young."

Daniel gazed at him with soft, kind eyes and Malcolm felt a tug at his chest. He did not like to think of his family, most especially his mother, but when this man's attention was upon him it was as if he could hold no secrets. Daniel laid his hand on Malcolm's and traced the skin across his knuckles.

A shimmer ran through Malcolm and made him heady. He cleared his throat. "And you," said Malcolm, wanting to talk not of himself. "What of your parents?"

"My parents?"

Daniel's arms fell by his side. He blinked and, standing straight, walked over by the fire. He leaned against the mantle and stared into the flames, silent for a few moments.

"No one has ever asked about my parents before." Malcolm came closer.

"Surely," he said gently. "You must have parents."

Daniel nodded.

"Only it has been so long I barely remember their faces." He took the stick and poked at the fire, sending a shower of embers upward into the chimney. "I remember my mother had a very warm smile, and I was always very happy to see it. She taught me all her gifts—she had a hand for dyeing and showed me all the ways to work the dyes to give the best colors. She was a very strong woman and she had a head for many things. She could read and write and even sometimes acted as a midwife for the women in the village."

"The herbs," said Malcolm.

"Yes. She was the most remarkable woman—person—I have ever known. She seemed to be able to master anything she tried. Of course, any woman who is too intelligent or too capable has a hard time in this world. Still, she had an iron backbone—unbreakable even until the end. And she could work cloth like no other."

"Both your parents were weavers then?"

Daniel leaned against the wall.

"Yes," he said. "It runs in the family, on both sides, for generations back."

"Have they also both passed away?"

Daniel nodded. "A very long time ago now."

"You must have been very young when they died."

"Young enough," he said with a shrug.

"After which you came to live with your grandfather? Did he also help you develop your talents?"

Daniel gave a sad smile. "What talents I have are his."

He shed his coat and bent to undo his boot laces.

"My parents were murdered," he said matter-of-factly.

Malcolm blinked in surprise. "Murdered? Both of them?"

"Yes." Daniel kicked off one boot and then moved on to the next. "They were falsely accused by some villagers of a certain crime. They were tortured. When they did not admit to the charges against them, they were both hanged. Or they were meant to be. My mother was to be hanged first but when they came to retrieve her, my father attacked the guards and was run through by their long knives. My mother died alone on the rope."

"My god. How horrid."

"Yes, it was," said Daniel softly as he stood. "But I suppose for the best."

"For the best?" exclaimed Malcolm.

"For my mother, I mean," said Daniel, moving across the room towards Malcolm. "The torture left her crippled, her hands mangled. If she had lived, the rest of her life would have been a torment. Being kept from the ability to do the things she cherished would have driven her mad. She was not a woman to be still and silent."

Daniel was in front of him now. He shrugged off the braces over his own shirt and let them fall to his sides. He reached up to tug at Malcolm's coat.

"Come now, my handsome stranger, I did not seek you out to wallow in misery. Not on a night like tonight. We must enjoy the beauty of the moon and its pull."

His hands settled on Malcolm's waist.

"Do you not feel its power work in your own nature?"

Malcolm certainly felt his body respond to Daniel's touch.

"Yes," he whispered.

"Good," said Daniel.

He took Malcolm by the hand and led him to the bed where they both sat. Malcolm bent to make quick work of his boots and when he sat back up Daniel began to undo the buttons of his waistcoat. While the young man's fingers worked, Malcolm finished removing his cravat, already loose from the evening's frolics.

Daniel swiftly removed the waistcoat and ran his hands down Malcolm's arms, feeling the hard knots of muscles there. Daniel tugged at Malcolm's shirt, loosening it from his trousers, and pulled it up. He ran his hands underneath the material, his fingers playing against the lines and curves of Malcolm's chest. Malcolm hissed an intake of breath, the touch like fire against his skin.

Malcolm reached out and pulled Daniel's mouth to his own. Their tongues danced together and he heard Daniel moan slightly. He released him and nipped at his bottom lip, smiling.

"You are not at all afraid," said Daniel, smiling himself.

"Afraid of what?"

"Of me. Many men are very wary when they come to my home of an evening."

"I assure you, I am not afraid of such things. I have spent many an evening with a man. Though few as lovely as you."

He ran a finger down Daniel's cheek and Daniel smiled.

"I have no shame in how I conduct my affairs," continued Malcolm. "But I am well aware of the discretion society demands. And the danger. But fear? It serves no good."

Daniel began to pull Malcolm's shirt over his head.

"Yours must be a very gilded existence not to worry about such things," he said. "Most do not have the status or wealth to protect themselves."

"Perhaps so. I admit I may have more influence than most. But it is still dangerous. No man is completely immune from the law nor the rabid crowd."

"You seem almost proud."

Malcolm wrapped his arms around the young man and pulled him close.

"Why should I not be proud? Even if they burn me at the stake, they cannot take away my soul. No matter what little spells they spill from those scrolls they call religion. And if my soul can never be taken, that is all that matters. I will continue to own myself."

There was a waver in Daniel's expression that Malcolm could not read. But it vanished as he kissed Malcolm again—a kiss sweeter than any Malcolm had ever tasted.

"Fine words," said Daniel. "That might change if you felt the flames licking your calves."

"Words matter far less than conviction. And they hardly ever align, for better or worse. And," he added with a wicked smile, "if I sin by the sword then I die by the sword. If I am to fall, then by the sword is the preferred method."

Daniel shook his head, amused. He moved to the floor and began to undo the fastenings of Malcolm's fall front.

"Hopefully you are more skilled in swordplay than you are in wordplay."

"Was that so terrible a pun?"

"Yes. Terrible."

He pulled Malcolm's trousers and small clothes down below his knees and leant in, taking Malcolm into his mouth. It was an exquisite sensation and Malcolm arched back onto his elbows, letting a loud moan escape his lips. He peered down at the man with the skilled mouth, and behind him, the light of the hearth seemed to fill the room as bright as daylight. He turned his head as he fell back onto the bed, and his eye caught a fold of crimson material nearby. He wondered for a moment at how difficult it was to achieve such brilliant shades of red. The light from the fire spilled over the silken wool and it seemed to shimmer and ripple in the darkness like the flames of the devil. All thought quickly dissipated as he was again awash in the wave of pleasure brought on by Daniel. Malcolm closed his eyes and gave in to it.

Afterwards, they lay on the bed, a pillow beneath them and the counterpane tangled about their legs. Malcolm rested his head against Daniel's chest, playing with a necklace Daniel wore. It was a band of silver, plain except for an engraved design of what appeared to be a rowan tree in its center, which Daniel wore around his neck on a piece of plain string.

"What is this ring?" Malcolm asked, twirling it in his fingers.

"Too long a story to tell," Daniel said, clasping his hand over Malcolm's and stilling it.

Malcolm turned to the hearth; as still yet it burned bright, its warmth reaching far across the room.

"I have never seen a fire burn so heartily," he murmured.

Daniel stroked his hair and hummed; the humming turned into a soft song.

"Ay! I did see a great lad I once loved," he sang.

"There by the roadside stood his smiling face,
A sight I should thought I twould ne'er be graced...."

"That song," Malcolm interrupted. "I know it well. My nanny used to sing it to me when I was young.

On the line, *Oh but his curls were lovely and silken*, she would sing the word 'milky' instead of silken."

"Milky?"

"Yes, it was her pet name for me. First from Malky then Milky Malky." He smiled, remembering her sing-song voice calling out little rhymes and games.

"It is a sad song though for a nursery, is it not? The lad with the silken locks dies at the end."

"Well, she was Irish, after all." Malcolm gave a little shrug. "She brought it with her from back home, she said. I am quite surprised you know it."

"These folk songs do travel. I'm sure it is centuries old by now, re-written many times over."

"Yes, probably so."

"Did you love your nanny very much?"

"Oh yes, very much. I suppose it is a hackneyed story. Young boy loses his mother and turns to the nursery for a caring bosom."

Malcolm paused.

"I believe, in a way, it was easier for my family. They never talked of my mother's humble background and, in fact, my grandparents invented an entirely new history for her that her death sealed as fact, not myth. I was taught never to speak of her to others, and soon, I felt as I had begun to forget who she actually was. She became like a woman of myth—remote and mysterious, powerful and beautiful, but only seen in my dreams, not the real world. Even now I only really think of her when I am alone with my own thoughts."

"You too have known much sorrow."

"Have I? I suppose so. But it is only life and its workings. We muddle our way through it." He reached up and ran his hand along Daniel's cheek. "I cannot imagine how you bear the sorrows you have suffered."

Daniel kissed his fingertips.

"I find that the longer you live, the easier it is to forget them."

"Really? I find exactly the opposite to be true. They are not the same stab of pain as they were years ago but the memories stay and sometimes arrive at the most unexpected of times to confuse you."

They were silent for a moment.

"I have never talked on my feelings of my mother and family with anyone," said Malcolm. "But with you, I must admit, it feels like confession, as if I were listing my life for absolution."

"Perhaps it is only the drink," said Daniel, moving in to kiss his neck. "Or the warmth of the fire."

Malcolm pushed back against his tightly muscled frame and craned his head, exposing the full length of his neck.

"Or the warmth of your body against mine," he said, his voice heavy.

"Or that," said Daniel.

He fluttered kisses against Malcolm's neck and then traced the line lightly with his fingertips.

"Such smooth, beautiful skin," he whispered as his touches moved past Malcolm's neck and circled around his chest. "So soft and unlined."

Malcolm hummed in reply, his eyes closed and a smile on his lips.

"Sleep now, dear Malky," said Daniel. "You have exerted yourself muchly tonight. Rest."

Chapter Eleven

M alcolm awoke to the sound of metal clatter-
ing. Blinking, he saw Daniel standing halfway
between the hearth and the bed, his naked body,
trembling, silhouetted by the fire. The expression
on his face seemed one of pure anguish.

"Daniel?" Malcolm tried to quell a rising ill-feel-
ing. "Is something the matter?"

Daniel closed his eyes briefly and turned away,
moving to the table nearby. He flopped into a chair,
the fire bright, throwing him into half silhouette. He
leaned an elbow on the table, covering his eyes, his
other arm hung loosely at his side.

Malcolm sat up. A glint of light caught his eye as
he did so, and glancing towards it, he saw a knife
lying on the floor near the hearth. The blade was
thin and curved, the edge shining, razor-like, as if
it had been recently sharpened. The sound that had
woken him must have been its falling. What had
prompted Daniel to take up a knife?

Instinct told him to divorce himself from this
circumstance immediately, although he struggled
to understand the sudden turn of atmosphere. He
had had many an encounter where men turned

violent after lovemaking, upset by the shame of their own urges. He had endured bellowing and curses, even bouts of fisticuffs, but the way Daniel had looked at him spoke of something different. Something seemingly tender and broken, and even more frightening than the usual. He pulled on his discarded trousers as he stood, grabbing the rest of his clothing.

Daniel sat in the chair, his arms wrapped around his midsection, bent over as if in pain. Yet his face, what Malcolm could see of it, was placid, almost stonily calm. It was a disquieting sight and it moved him. Against his better judgment, Malcolm laid his hand on the man's shoulder. When Daniel lifted his face, it was strained and creased with consternation. He appeared aged, years older, best by torturesome emotions.

"You should go."

Malcolm was taken aback. "This very minute?"

"Yes, go. Now."

"Have I done something to offend you, Daniel?"

"It isn't that." He gritted his teeth. "I can offer no promises."

"I haven't asked for any promises."

"You don't understand. At dawn ..." Daniel faltered. He sat upright and unfolded his arms. His ragged breath escaped him. "My grandfather will return at dawn."

"And you don't want him to see me here?"

"He cannot."

"I understand, believe me. I have dealt with many an angry parent in my day, or spouse come to that."

Malcolm knew all too well the hazards of guilty men. "But dawn is hours off yet. Surely it cannot be as urgent as that."

Daniel shook his head, grimacing.

"No, now is better. You must go now. My grandfather—I can't guarantee—I'm not sure what he would do. He has been known to be... aggressive."

"Surely an old man can't be—"

"Violent. Sometimes he is violent. Especially when dawn comes."

"Where has he been? Out drinking? What keeps him away all night?"

"No, not drink." Daniel turned away then, a queer expression on his face. "The moon."

"The moon?" Malcolm pulled on his shirt, baffled. "What has the moon to do with anything?"

"Strange things happen on a moon like this," Daniel said, his voice as even as still water. "Strange and powerful things. There is a power in the moon."

Malcolm knelt beside him. Daniel turned away from him and stared into the fire. Malcolm ran his fingers through the hair at Daniel's temples.

"No," Daniel objected with a whisper but he did not stop Malcolm's caresses.

"The type of thing you spoke of at the lake?"

"Yes."

Malcolm searched the face of the beautiful man he'd just lain with. Daniel's eyes closed as Malcolm stroked his hair.

"Something like magic?" asked Malcolm.

Daniel's eyes snapped open and he glared at Malcolm, a hard, frantic stare.

"You must go. I beg you." Daniel brought a clenched fist to his lips, hiding his mouth. "Please."

"I promise I will not give you reason to be at odds with your grandfather."

Malcolm was weary and better sense told him the young man was clearly troubled, yet something called on him to stay. He wanted to wrap Daniel up in his arms, to stave off whatever this wild, piercing panic was. He wanted to protect him, to save him.

Daniel cupped his hand under Malcolm's chin. Daniel's expression was blank, his eyes like two rounds of polished flint, black and glistening, as he turned Malcolm's head from side to side, studying his face.

"So young," whispered Daniel.

A cold feeling sprung up in Malcolm's stomach.

"I'm older than you, hardly young," he stammered.

"You do not understand," said Daniel, his voice hollow and ragged. Suddenly he grasped Malcolm by the neck. "You understand nothing."

His voice was not loud but it had such intensity that it felt like a shout.

His hand tightened around Malcolm's neck.

"D-d-Daniel," Malcolm sputtered in protest.

But Daniel did not seem to hear. His face was a mask, his eyes dark, the spaces around them hollowed and shadowed. His cheeks seemed sunken, his nostrils flared. His grip was like a vice closing and he stood, wrenching Malcolm up by the neck. Once Malcolm was on his feet, Daniel began to push him, driving him backward, and Malcolm tripped over his own feet. But Daniel held him by the throat, his arm extended at full length, and he kept pressing Malcolm back and back.

The skin on Daniel's face seemed to stretch taught against the bones, his eyes like two pools of pure black. His lips parted in a hideous smile, and when he spoke his voice seemed amplified, as if more than one person spoke, multiple times converged into one roar of sound.

"YOU. MUST. LEAVE."

Malcolm's vision went blurry and the air struggled to fill his lungs.

"GO," Daniel's voice again rang out.

Suddenly there was a hard smack as he hit the wall. Daniel's grip released and Malcolm fell to the floor gasping and rubbing at his throat.

Daniel stumbled back and fell to his knees, his body limp.

"I'm sorry," he cried, his voice filled with desperation. "I'm so sorry, sorry, sorry."

He began to weep.

Malcolm's head swam, he felt addled. Even though every good sense in his body told him to run, to flee this man who had only seconds ago had him clawing for breath, he instead moved towards him. The sound of weeping shook something far deeper in Malcolm and he put his arm around Daniel, pulling him to his chest. He buried his face in Daniel's hair.

"I'm so sorry." Daniel's sobs began to ease. "But you must go. Please. I beg of you."

Malcolm nodded, knowing that no comfort could come. He jumped up, retrieved his boots and pulled them on quickly.

At the door, he turned.

Daniel was still on the floor, naked and huddled. He had brought his knees up to his chest and buried his face against them. Only the light falling through the window from outside hit him and it cast his skin a somber pale blue.

It was a sorrowful and delicate sight that made Malcolm want to pick Daniel up, to cradle him, hold him close and comfort him with kisses. A chorus of chaos rang out in his mind. Pain, fear, confusion, anger—all bounced around in a cacophony. He shut his eyes, sighing deeply, and shook his head. He pushed the door open and felt the cold midnight rush in around him. He welcomed its bracing touch and stepped out. Letting his feet swiftly carry him, he willed himself not to look back at the lonely cottage, worried he might again reconsider.

Back in his room over the tavern, he poured some frigid water into the basin and splashed his face. He undressed and got into bed, grateful to see his hot water bottle had not yet cooled. He pulled the blanket up to his chin, and for the first time since he left the tavern that evening, he felt somewhat clear-headed. As he had moved through the darkened forest back to the tavern he had been plagued by the feeling that he had forgotten or abandoned something. Even as he struggled to make sense of what had happened in the weaver's cottage, the images of Daniel's scowling face, the fire, and the discarded knife had begun to fade. What he remembered most vividly, with utmost clarity, was two competing images. Daniel's face above him in bed, his hair lit brightly by the firelight, and the sorrowful pose of him on the floor, blue as a megrim, the shadows of night enveloping him.

As he finally drifted to sleep, he hoped it would all make more sense in the daylight.

Chapter Twelve

B reakfast was a slab of fried ham, some stewed fruit and a piece of fried dough. He tore through it, more ravenous than he had been in some time, and ate hardly tasting the food. He ordered a second plateful and was rewarded with an extra slice of fried dough, Mrs. Beamon, the mistress of the inn, being delighted in what she took as a compliment to her cooking. He was just tucking in when the tavern door opened and a trio of rough-looking fellows made their way in, clamoring for ale.

"You know I serve naught but small beer before sunset," Mrs. Beamon admonished them. And though they grumbled, they happily partook.

Malcolm did not recognize them from the preceding evening, and they struck him as the types better avoided, judging by the hard glances thrown his way as they settled around a nearby table.

He tried to ignore their presence and sipped his own small beer, thinking on the day ahead. If he left before midday he would have time to make it home by dark, even sparing a small detour to the weaver's cottage. He did not desire to disturb Daniel but he could not shake the despair born from those last moments in the cottage. Despite the warnings of this vicious grandfather who must now be returned, he needed to know that Daniel was safe. That the night had not left him shattered. And a lovely bolt of crimson material would be just the gift to return to his sister with, so trade gave him an excuse for a visit.

A commotion at the door interrupted his thoughts. He looked up to see a young woman entering with a basket on her arm. One of the men who had been glaring at Malcolm stood, holding his cap to his chest.

"On my good lord, Alse Staughton," he declared, waggling his eyebrows at the young woman, "you are a diamond of the first water."

"And you, Elias Rawthorn," she replied with a grimace of disgust, "are a tap-hackled old goat of a lecher. Be quiet with you."

Elias' cronies cried out in laughter and he fell into his chair, feigning a wound. As Elias leaned back, he turned his head in Malcolm's direction. He sneered at Malcolm, his lip lifting to expose two blackened front teeth. Malcolm set his jaw and leaned forward on the table, returning the menacing expression.

"Oh, it will look just magnificent," cried Mrs. Beamon, distracting both men.

Alse smiled and nodded. In her arms, she held a folded length of material, pale green in color with a surface that shone like silk. Grandly, Alse let a fold on the material fall in front of her, resting against her body. Mrs. Beamon beamed in appreciation and ran the back of her hand against the soft surface.

"With her coloring and hair, I think it would be the perfect complement," said Alse. "I cannot wait to begin making it."

"Where did you get that, you wet goose?" Elias called out.

Alse grimaced at Mrs. Beamon and rolled her eyes.

"You know well where I got it," she replied, without sparing a glance at Elias.

"You will regret frolicking with that heathen, that you will, Alse Staughton. You ought to keep a keen eye before you are sullied yourself."

"I shall regret many a thing in my life, I am sure," answered Alse. "Most especially entertaining the talk of empty-headed frogs such as I see before me. But I shall never regret trading with Old Man Weaver."

"He's a sinner!" cried Elias.

Alse put her hand on her hip and leveled him with a look.

"And what of you? Deep in your cups at every hour of the day? Cast not stones, Elias Rawthorn."

"Don't you chastise me, you wench. I am old enough to be your father. And you should be grateful that someone cares about your soul."

"I should be grateful that we have such a craftsman among us. He's the nearest point I have within a day's ride, and he is willing to trade for far less than his handiwork is worth. And, come to that, you beef wit, he weaves the most beautiful fabric. He has the touch of an artist."

"He has the touch of Lucifer, he has," said Elias. "He should have been made to kiss the rope long ago."

"Let it lay," interceded Mrs. Beamon. "The old man does no harm. 'Tis but him and his loom in that old cottage, and he hardly sees another soul."

"But what of his grandson?" Malcolm surprised even himself in speaking up. But the thought of discussing the very man who had consumed his thoughts all morning was too much.

Elias Rawthorn shot up from his chair and turned towards Malcolm. Mrs. Beamon exchanged a concerned glance with Alse.

"What do you know of his grandson?" asked Elias, his tone rough and threatening.

Malcolm regretted speaking, but he knew better than to be cowed by a type like Elias.

"Only that I met him last night."

"Met him?" Elias erupted. He moved swiftly towards Malcolm's table. He slammed his fists down on its top. "And where did you meet this creature?"

Malcolm calmly took a sip of his small beer before he answered.

"Here," he replied, looking up at Elias, his tone cool. "Just outside this very tavern."

Mrs. Beamon gasped.

Elias leaned farther forward, the stench of his breath hitting Malcolm in the face.

"And did you follow this man to his cottage?" he asked with a sneer.

Malcolm was suddenly alert. Had he been seen leaving with Daniel? Who could possibly have known where they went? But he did not let his doubt show. He stood, shoving the table forward roughly and knocking Elias back so that he almost lost his footing.

"You will watch your filthy mouth," Malcolm roared. He pushed aside his topcoat and laid his hand on his pistol.

Mrs. Beamon rushed forward.

"None of that!" she cried. She turned to Malcolm. "Elias has the tongue of a loose fish, to be sure, and I do apologize for his coarse and rude words, but your tale is disconcerting here."

"Exchanging pleasantries with a stranger is a tale disconcerting?" Malcolm asked. "Madam, you confuse me."

"Not a stranger, my lord," said Mrs. Beamon, still watching him with a wary eye. "With a witch."

"A witch?" exclaimed Malcolm. "What are these nursery tales you spin?"

"This grandson you speak of," spat Elias, "is the old man himself."

Malcolm stared at Elias; he felt a coldness grip his insides.

"Ridiculous," he managed to say.

"He is only ever seen during the harvest moon," offered Mrs. Beamon. "When it is said Old Man Weaver takes the form of a beautiful young man and roams the woods."

"Looking for fresh sacrifices," added Elias.

The discarded knife by the fire. And yet he had escaped—had been forced to go, in fact, by Daniel.

It did not signify. Malcolm stood mutely, searching the faces that watched him.

"Well, I think you're all telling Banbury stories." The bright voice of Alse punctured the silence. Malcolm was grateful for her interruption; confusion reigned in his mind. "I've never seen such fine work in all my life. And Old Man Weaver has never been anything but kind to me. All these foul words are nothing but nonsense."

"'Tis not nonsense, little girl," croaked a voice from the corner of the room.

All turned to the look at the old woman there. She was an ancient specimen, her skin as lined and dark as the walls of the tavern. Her lids hung low and Malcolm would have declared her aslumber if she had not spoken. Her gnarled hands clasped the head of a thick walking stick, polished until it shone.

"Old Man Weaver has signed the Devil's book as sure as the water runs through the river, and I am sure of it," she declared.

"How can you be so sure?" asked Alse.

"The old man appeared in our village when my own mam was but a young sapling and I a new babe at her side. Yet here he has remained the whole of my own life, and I've not seen the dawn of youth in anyone's remembrance. He told us that he came from somewhere in East Anglia, where he had made his trade as a weaver like his father and his grandfather before him. But my mam and those who lived here then came upon the knowledge that many a weaver had been driven from that very area by the Witchfinder General himself and that they had been made to wander all over the countryside seeking out refuge and new homes."

"You don't mean the Witchfinder Matthew Hopkins?" asked Malcolm, incredulous.

"Aye, but I do, young man. Many of those cast out were caught along the way and killed for the black practitioners they were, but some did escape. And they moved on and on, traveling alone, finding villages to attach themselves to, draining them of life and faith."

"That seems beyond fathoming, grandmother," said Malcolm. "The Witchfinder General has been dead for almost two hundred years."

The old woman gave a sharp shake of her head.

"Do a one of you remember a time when Old Man Weaver has not lived in this village?" she asked, looking around the tavern. "Nay, you do not. And do you a one of you remember him when he was not old and grey? Nay, you do not."

"But how is that possible?" asked Malcolm.

"Because he is a witch," she answered with a small downward jerk of her cane so that it struck the wooden floor like a judge's gavel. "There are those who visit our hamlet. They come on the night of a harvest moon in the shadow of Mabon, stopping here, for respite or relief." She waved her hand, fanning out her fingers. "And then they disappear like morning dew from the grass. Gone. Leaving behind all they carried—their coin, their clothing, their horses, their carriages, everything a man needs. Abandoned."

She cast her rheumy eyes on Malcolm.

"And they are all last seen in the company of a young man with flame-colored hair."

Malcolm froze, feeling as if his body was suddenly made of stone. He wanted to admonish the old woman, tell her that she was a fabulist and full of superstition. He wanted to laugh in the faces of them all. Yet he could not shake the queer feeling that had overtaken him—that he had somehow managed to escape the very fate of which she spoke.

From across the room, Alse guffawed.

"Silence, you beef-wit," barked Elias. "What do you know of anything in this world?"

Alse pursed her lips tightly and looked as if she might spit.

"I have a wedding dress to make," she declared. "I know that much if nothing more. You may all wallow in the mire of your superstitious tales, but I'd rather see how life goes on. You moan about murder and curses, but I have something of love to occupy me."

She gathered up her basket and headed for the door.

"I too must take my leave," said Malcolm, shaken from his mental freeze. "You have left me with much fat to chew on during my journey, but I must get home before dark. My horse is packed for the ride, and I have family waiting on me. Mrs. Beamon, if you will allow me to settle my bill."

He did so, feeling all eyes watching him. Mrs. Beamon handed him his change and he thanked her for her hospitality and made to leave. As he neared the door, he felt a hand grab his arm. It was Elias, suddenly beside him.

"Perhaps it is you," said Elias, his voice heavy.

"What?"

"Perhaps you are the one sent to free us of the curse," ventured Elias. "Perhaps you are the one who was sent to destroy him finally."

Malcolm recoiled from the naked entreaty in the man's gaze. He wrenched free his arm of Elias' grip.

"I wish you a good day, sir."

Once astride Grannus, although his mind was a clutter of so many thoughts and feelings, there was no longer a debate. Under the guise of trade or no, he must visit the weaver's cottage. He must see for himself whether there was only the old man or if Daniel remained as well. Common sense told him that, of course, they would both be in residence. These people were clearly completely entrenched in their superstitions and backwards beliefs—only Alse seemed to have a shred of clear-mindedness. So far-fetched were their assertions that he wondered if it had not clouded their sanity, if perhaps they had been too far removed for too long out here, so that even the appearance of a stranger caused a queer pandemonium of emotion. No wonder these former visitors were never heard from or seen again; Malcolm imagined they had likely fled the strange village as quickly as possible. If Elias and his lot were any indication, there might have been quite a fear of brutalization or attack felt in the breast of any stranger.

And yet for as much as he yearned to dismiss their fables and speculation, he could not shake the feeling of seeing Daniel so exposed the previous

evening. He had been wracked with a battle of emotions such that Malcolm had never witnessed before—his manner, his body, his voice, the whole experience seemed almost otherworldly. He could not
deny that somehow the man had seemed possessed,
of a sorrow, yes, but something far deeper than even
that. Something that tore at his very soul. A decision
had been made last night in that cottage; a decision,
that if the villagers were to be believed, might have
spared Malcolm his life. But why? And to what end?
He knew how moved he had been by his time with
Daniel, how he had felt for a few hours a rare comfort. When he had lain with Daniel, when he had
cradled him in his arms, he felt no worry, no hurts
of past heartaches, no troubling thoughts of future
duties. He could talk freely of his childhood, of his
beloved mother, of all the things that had shaped the
man he had become, and yet he registered no injury,
no judgment. He had felt, for perhaps the first time
he could remember, completely and utterly free,
unencumbered by the expectations of the world.

Chapter Thirteen

H e saw the bent trees that announced the entrance to the small cove by the lake where the weaver's cottage stood. He brought Grannus to a slow trot and moved closer, hesitantly but determined. Though a few trees lay in his vision, he could see the cottage as well as the figure outside of it. It was an old man with a walking stick. He was bent with age and moved slowly across the pathway outside the cottage. His feet padded along the ground; his clothing, though not newly fashioned, was neat and clean and well-made and yet it hung off his slight, gnarled frame, almost shapeless in its need for flesh. Malcolm could not clearly make out his face, but even at a distance, he could see the many lines of age and the thin, sallow skin that hung about his face and neck. He appeared even more wizened and worn than the old woman in the tavern.

He watched as the old man stopped to pick a flower or weed from the ground and had to lower himself delicately and slowly. Malcolm imagined that he heard the creaking of his joints from even here. This was the Old Man Weaver he had been warned of? This was the man who, among the flood of moonlight of a harvest moon, was magically transformed into the straight-backed, strong, beautiful man he knew as Daniel? So overcome with shock and surprise was he that Malcolm wanted to laugh. Surely, he told himself, he had let his mind run like a wild animal, crashing through good sense and true, sound thinking. How in all imagining could this frail, decrepit man be a threat of any sort; hold any type of power or dominion over the forces of nature? He felt a fool for being so swayed by those ale-fed ghost stories. Surely there must be some other reason Daniel had pushed him away in the night. It could not be fear of this poor man. He was determined to speak to Daniel himself and find out the answer.

Malcolm clicked his tongue and urged Grannus closer to the cottage. The old man, obviously hearing their approach, turned towards rider and horse and examined them. Suddenly, Grannus came to a complete stop in the middle of the clearing. Grannus was a strong horse with steady nerves and did not spook easily, and his reaction surprised Malcolm. He murmured encouragement to his steed but Grannus would go no further. Malcolm patted his neck and dismounted.

"Excuse me, sir," he called out, after quickly tying Grannus to a nearby makeshift post.

The old man turned away and offered no reply.

"I do not mean to disturb," called Malcolm. "But I wondered if I might inquire as to something."

The old man did not turn but held up his free hand.

"I am taking no bespoke orders at the moment, sir.
"

His voice was throaty and smoky with age, but there was something familiar about it.

"I did hope to purchase some of your cloth work. I have seen it in the village and it is truly well-turned. But there is more I want to ask."

The old man stopped and lifted his head, but still did not turn.

"You have seen my cloth in the village?"

"Yes, a young woman brought some into the tavern in which I was staying."

"Ah, young Alse. And she was happy with it?" he asked.

"Yes, very much. All who saw it complimented her on its quality."

The old man nodded.

"That is good. It is meant to be a wedding dress."

"Yes, so she said."

"She will make a fine garment of it, by no doubt. She has the magic in her hands. She is one of the few. I am glad to hear it. Garments of love deserve attention."

The old man began to move towards the cottage.

"Sir, if you might allow me another question."

The old man continued to shuffle.

"I have come about Daniel."

The old man stopped. Slowly, using his stick to guide him, he turned to face Malcolm. When he saw the face of the old man in full, Malcolm's throat went dry.

"He's gone," the old man said shortly and turned away.

Malcolm was thrown and tried to remain sensible.

"Gone?" asked Malcolm. "Shall he return?"

"No," said the old man waving his hand. "Never again."

"But, sir, how so? It has only been a few hours—that is, the day is quite young. How far could he have gone since dawn?"

Malcolm stepped forward to follow the old man.

"You will not find him again," the old man declared. He tried to shuffle faster. "Now you must—"

The old man was interrupted by his own cry as, in his haste, his walking stick hit an uneven ridge of earth and went out from under him. Malcolm rushed forward to help him. He caught him by the arm and the old man turned up his face towards Malcolm. His expression read of panic and fear, true, but also a fear far deeper than that of a fall. Malcolm's mind filled with images of Daniel, shadowed by the blaze of the hearth at night. His drawn, agonized face as he looked up from the chair. His body sprawled on the cottage floor, prostrate in the moonlight.

Perhaps you are the one sent to free us of the curse.

The remembered words of Elias Rawthorn in his mind struck him like a slap in the face.

"Please, sir," he said. "Let me help you."

Trembling, the old man nodded.

"Can I take you inside?" Malcolm asked.

"No," the old man said sharply. "No, no, here is fine."

He waved his hand towards a small stool that sat just outside the entrance to the cottage which Malcolm helped him lower himself on to.

"My stick."

Malcolm retrieved it and handed it over. The old man settled the stick across his lap and Malcolm noticed that his hands still shook.

"You are Old Man Weaver?"

"As I am called," he answered, casting a suspicious eye up at Malcolm. "What business do you have with me?"

Malcolm dropped to one knee, feeling unsure. Dare he broach the suspicions he had in his mind? Dare he confront this ancient soul and demand answers?

"Good sir, I do not mean to molest or harass you by any account. In truth, I only hoped to speak with your grandson Daniel once more before I left. I had a mind to thank him. He showed me great hospitality and kindness during my stay in this village." Malcolm straightened his cuff. "Indeed, he showed me more hospitality than most anyone else I have ever met."

Old Man Weaver studied him.

"And that is the only reason you come?"

Malcolm looked up. "What other reason could I have?"

"Ill-will. Suspicion. Destruction. Those are the usual visitors in this place."

"Sir, I have no such things in my heart for this place, and most especially not for Daniel."

The old man's eyes widened for a moment and then he dropped his chin to his chest.

"As I said, he has gone."

"Would it be possible to wait for his return?" asked Malcolm.

Old Man Weaver shook his head.

"He will not return."

"Surely he will be back at some point? Maybe if not today, then some other day, a day perhaps when the atmosphere is more welcoming."

Weaver studied Malcolm. He moved his lips as if to speak, but they began to tremble and turned his face away.

"It is only me here now," he said after a moment's silence. He faced Malcolm, his eyes sharp. "Daniel will never return. And I should like to be left in peace. For what little time I have left."

Again Malcolm felt as if he had been slapped in the face. He stood, more tired than he had known he was. His body sagged as if he had suffered an injury or sudden defeat.

"Very well, sir. I certainly mean no offense, I'm sure. I have now grown quite accustomed to being turned away from this cottage, perplexed and confused. If you insist, I shall bother you no more. But I implore of you one last favor. If you do see Daniel again, if he ever returns in the future, some day, or month, or year from now—on a whim or by magic or if you suddenly see him appear in a pool of moonlight across the forest—will you tell him that Malcolm Robertson came to look for him? That I wanted to thank him for the kindness he showed me, and I only wished to somehow repay it. And, of most importance, please tell him that I hope to meet him again someday, to see him, if only briefly. Should he be so compelled, he can write to me at Farrington Hall, and I will gladly visit here or bring him there to stay with me if such a thing is possible. I would welcome a chance to know him further. In fact, if truth be said, I have never known a greater want in my life than to know him."

Weaver looked at him, silent, and Malcolm held his gaze. Tears were forming in the old man's eyes, tears that threatened to spill at any second. Those eyes as deeply green as any forest, with irises that flowed into a bottomless well, sparkling with youth despite the lines of age that surrounded them. Malcolm must know, he could not leave without knowing.

"It is you then, is it not?" he asked.

Those green eyes darkened and the old man dropped his head.

"I don't know what you mean," he said quietly.

"You are Daniel," declared Malcolm softly. "You must be. But how?"

"I am the Old Man Weaver," he protested weakly.

"Those eyes are the same ones I looked into before," said Malcolm. "They can be none other. You must be Daniel. But how?"

"Sir, I assure you—"

"So it is as they say then?" asked Malcolm, kneeling again before the old man. "That your practice magic? That you are a witch?"

Old Man Weaver's mouth was a tight line as if he willed himself not to speak. Finally, he conceded.

"That is the name they give it, yes."

"But if their stories are to be believed, you have lived many decades, centuries perhaps."

"Perhaps."

"And they say that you live so long by taking the lives of young men. By using their body and blood to sustain your own."

Weaver rested his hand on the walking stick and sighed.

"They know much, it seems, about the ways of a witch."

"But if this is true, how can it be so? It does not signify. The marvelous man I met last evening, he is not a thing of evil or treachery. He is by far a thing of beauty, something to make a man's heart sing."

Old Man Weaver looked at him, his eyes full of pain.

"You must go. Leave me be."

He righted himself, pushing himself up from the stool, and turned towards the house.

"No," demanded Malcolm. "You must tell me if it is true."

The old man shook his head.

"You must decide for yourself," he muttered.

Malcolm grabbed his arm and halted him. His grip was strong and, for a moment, he realized how frail the old man truly was. It felt as if he might snap into pieces with a single false move. Gingerly he turned him to face Malcolm.

"Tell me," he pleaded.

"You want to hear of hearts torn from their chests?" croaked the old man. "You want me to tell you of bodies laid bare, young souls discarded? Is this the knowledge you seek? If you want to destroy me, sir, you may do so. Easily, I imagine. But spare me the shame of storytelling."

Malcolm felt a tightness in his chest; he felt tears threaten.

"But why, if you are so powerful as to change form in the light of a harvest moon, would you use your powers in such a way?"

Old Man Weaver turned away from the anguish in his questions.

"Leave me be, I tell you."

"Is it simply vanity?" snapped Malcolm. "A want to live forever, to be immortal?"

"To live forever?" Old Man Weaver bit back. He cackled, a short dry laugh full of bitterness. "Why would I desire to live like this?" He snatched his arm from Malcolm's grasp. "Broken, half lame, a shell of a person. I am hardly alive when I breathe. And you talk to me of living forever?"

"Then why? You must explain to me why. I cannot reconcile the notion of such heinous acts with the tenderness and distress I found here only yesterday evening," said Malcolm. He lifted his head and felt a lump in his throat, suddenly overcome by the truth he had dared not acknowledge. "And why, I must know, if this all be true, was I spared?"

His voice was ragged, and it clearly moved Old Man Weaver to hear it so. He cast his eyes down, thoughtful for a moment.

"I must sit," he said and went into the cottage. "Come."

Malcolm found the small home no different than he had left it. In fact, it looked somehow more welcoming in the day. The fire no longer burned in the hearth and the sunlight poured through the large windows, suffusing all the contents with a warm glow. The fabric that hung in the loom which had so resembled the fires of hell in the night, was now cool and soft, like the soothing currents of a fresh river, in the daylight.

Old Man Weaver fell into one of the chairs by the table and motioned to the other. Malcolm obliged and sat across from him. Weaver was silent for some time, staring into the stone of the cold hearth. His eyes clouded over and when he finally began to speak, his voice lost all trace of the creaks and groans of old age. He spoke clearly, determinedly, in a low voice.

"Thomas was the most marvelous man I had ever seen when he came to our village with his family. Although his relatives were the sort to blend well, he always kept himself to himself and made few friends. Except for me. We took to each other instantly, and developed such a passion for one another's company, that little else mattered. Then one night, as we lay by the fire of my hearth, he confessed to me of his powers. And he knew, he assured me, that I too possessed them. Of course, I did, just like my parents before me, but I had done all I could to keep them hidden. I had barely escaped alive when my parents were murdered, and I had roamed the country for months and months until I found this place where I was not known and managed to settle in as a weaver. It was not an existence I wanted to abandon so easily.

"My heart was frozen with fear and I called him a liar. But he laughed at me and took me out into the woods, far from the village, where he showed me the truth of his abilities. From that night, bathed in the light of a blue moon, we became inseparable. He came to be my apprentice in weaving, or so he told anyone who asked, and we lived together in my cottage. In such good humor as I found myself, my talents began to bloom and my reputation flourished all around. Every village in want of good cloth came to ask for me. But the aunt of Thomas, with whom he had lived before, came to resent our bounty. She hissed foul words about the two of us living as man and wife and began to spread all manner of gossip and slander. Finally, from the story told by a visiting preacher who told the village of a family of weavers put to the rope for engaging in the dark arts some counties over, the aunt stained us with the accusation of witchcraft. If she had any clue to Thomas's real talents, and if she shared them herself, I never knew for, in the end, it did not matter. The way in which we lived, so together and so obviously enamored, was enough to warrant suspicions and despising in the minds of those around, even the ones who called us friends. Within days of her poisonous words, the whole village hunted us, chasing us from our home and out into the forest like wild hares destined for the butcher's knife.

"On the night of the harvest moon, so full and bright in the sky, as we fled from our newly discovered hiding place, we were separated. As the villagers stormed the forest, the night sky almost as bright as day, we ran and ran. They managed to find Thomas, and I hid in the shadows as they took him. I watched from afar, my lungs near bursting with wails of terror I could not free, as they put him to trial by water. I could do nothing; I did nothing. I *became* nothing in those shadows. As they tied the rope around his waist and tossed him into the rushing river, I was mute. A coward frozen in the brush."

He broke off then and went silent. He closed his eyes and dropped his head. Malcolm could feel the hot tears sting his own eyes and he wanted to throw his arms around the old man to comfort him. But before he could, Weaver began to speak again, his eyes still closed.

"They lay his limp body on a large stone by the side of the river. He had passed the trial with his death, and now they determined that the true witch was me. Like a passel of wild boar, they grunted and were off again so that I was forced to run and hide for all the hours of the night. Finally, at dawn, just when the sun was reaching over the horizon, they returned to the village to rest. I crept back to the river but I found the stone empty. All that lay there now was the silver ring, a rowan tree carved into the band, which was never free of Thomas' hand. And then I knew that he had not died, that somehow he had escaped. So I took the ring and made a silent promise to find him. To keep searching until we could be reunited."

Weaver lifted his head and reached into his tunic, pulling out the ring Malcolm recognized from the night before.

"All these years," he said. "I have lived to find him again. Using my powers to take the body and blood of the young was only that I might live another year, to go searching, traveling the countryside, that I might one day be reunited with him, my Thomas. I have grown so tired, so old and weary, that traveling is a burden. But I cannot abandon my hope."

Malcolm felt the tears roll down his cheeks.

"But after all this time," Malcolm said. "Surely he cannot still be alive?"

"Yet I am still alive," said Weaver fiercely.

"But at what cost?" rejoined Malcolm. "Could it not be that he did not survive, and only that his ring was left behind. You have dedicated your life to finding him, but the countryside is not so large. I cannot imagine that if he once knew the love of Daniel that he would not seek it out as fiercely as you have sought him."

"Then I have lived for nothing," croaked Weaver. "Nothing at all."

The light left the old man's eyes and he dropped the ring. It fell softly against his chest. He slumped in his chair.

Malcolm moved forward and knelt in front of Weaver. He took the man's hands in his.

"You must not despair," he told him but got no reply.

Malcolm reached up and lifted his chin. The man would not meet his eyes.

"Daniel," said Malcolm softly. "Oh, Daniel. Do not leave me so soon."

Weaver looked at him, his eyes flooded with tears.

"Love, dear Malky," he said, his voice barely a whisper. "Has been all I ever sought."

"And perhaps you have found it yet."

Malcolm leaned forward and pressed his lips against Weaver's lips. At first there was resistance, but finally, Weaver gave in. Malcolm closed his eyes and kissed him deeply, feeling the warmth of his tongue against the other, gently sliding his hand around Weaver's neck and caressing the back of his head. Lost in the warmth of their shared passion.

When he pulled back, he could not believe his eyes.

There before him in the chair was Daniel. Not Old Man Weaver, whose lips he had just kissed, but Daniel as he had known him the night before. His body youthful and strong, his titian hair full and gleaming, his countenance freed of lines and marks, save for those of the tears which streamed down his cheeks.

"Oh, Daniel," Malcolm exclaimed, lifting the man's hands to his mouth and kissing them.

When Daniel saw this, he pulled his hands back and studied them. Bewildered, his eyes sought Malcolm's.

"Am I?" he stuttered. "Could it be?"

"Yes," cried Malcolm, tears streaming through laughter. "You are young again."

Daniel brought his hands to his face and moved them around, touching his own skin, his lips, running his fingers through his hair. His eyes, brighter than ever, gleamed with joy.

"There was a reason then, that you spared me," said Malcolm. "That you could not bring yourself to sacrifice me for another year of life. That you abandoned your search for Thomas."

Daniel's expression was a mix of joy and pain.

"I could not say it," he gasped. "I could not admit it to myself. I did not think it could be true."

"Oh, my, Daniel, but it is true. You found love after all. And now, it seems, some sort of curse has been broken."

"But how can this be so?" asked Daniel. "How can you love me too, after all the things I have told you, after all the horrible things I have done?"

"Maybe I should not," admitted Malcolm. "Yet I do. Perhaps it is because this world is a cruel place. All you sought was love, and at every turn, you had it snatched from you, taken away, destroyed. Yet you found a way to keep living, so that you might find it again somehow, in some way. It is perhaps not beautiful, but it is life, and now you—we—have been given a new chance at it."

"What if they come again?" asked Daniel, breathless. "To destroy us again?"

"No one will ever destroy you, or our love, ever again. I will see to that," declared Malcolm.

He put his hands on the face of his beloved titian-haired boy and brought their lips together, kissing him and already dreaming of days to come.

They were happy together for many, many years to come at Farrington Hall.

Daniel abandoned his weaving, for it too closely reminded him of the many years spent embroiled in his search for ongoing life. Eventually, he returned to the healing arts which his mother had taught him and became known all around the county for his ability to cure the ailing and to midwife as well as any woman ever had.

And although they never spoke of the past, Malcolm never forgot that first fateful night in the weaver's cottage, its hearth blazing like a beacon, a guidepost to somewhere new and undiscovered.

They never saw the village again. Even as they rode the same journey back and forth visiting the estate of Malcolm's great aunt. Even when later the railroad had been put in, and Malcolm's sister inherited that same estate and their many trips were instead to visit her. Even when a rail stop was added not but two miles from where the village must have stood, they saw no evidence of it. The ticket seller, the conductor, the local woman selling flowers on the platform, not a one had ever heard of a village in that forest so near with bent trees like great columns, despite Malcolm's occasional inquiries. Daniel never spoke of the place, or, in fact, his past at all—and Malcolm never asked him. It wasn't until the grey tinge of age began showing at Daniel's auburn temples that Malcolm realized he had never even asked the name of the seemingly vanished place. It was almost as if Daniel's life had begun on the day when Malcolm had pulled him up on Grannus' back, outside the weaver's cottage, and they had followed the path out of the forest, not turning back.

Though sometimes, as the great steam train rattled over the tracks, Malcolm caught Daniel looking out of the train window. His eyes fixed on the land where the village had once lain, and Malcolm saw a wistfulness come into his expression. But then Daniel would turn to Malcolm and smile brightly and the melancholy would dissipate.

Malcolm would take Daniel's hand in his own and give it a squeeze.

And if no one was near he might lift that same hand and bless it with a kiss.

Author's Note

Thank you for reading! If you have the time to share your thoughts with other readers by leaving a review of this or any other work by Joshua Ian, it would be greatly appreciated. Reviews help boost visibility, which is of utmost importance for independent authors. Feel free to leave your thoughts on Goodreads, Bookbub, or wherever you purchased this eBook.

MOODY BOXFAN

BOOKS

Copyright

Editing by Deborah Nemeth
Deborah Nemeth Editing Services

Additional Editing by Sue Laybourn
No Stone Unturned Editing Services
http://nostoneunturnedediting.co.uk/

Cover design by Dar Albert

Wicked Smart Designs
https://www.wickedsmartdesigns.com/

The Harvest Moon
Copyright © 2019 by Joshua Ian
Published by Moody Box Fan Books
ISBN: 978-1-7334803-0-7 (e-book version)

Editing by Sue Laybourn
No Stone Unturned Editing Services
http://nostoneunturnedediting.co.uk/

About the Author

Joshua Ian can easily be captured by a witty turn of phrase or a low-bottomed electronic bassline. If you manage to combine the two, then you have his heart forever. He lives in New York City and is a keen cinema lover and self-proclaimed *Dark Chocolate Expert*. When not staring at a blank screen and cursing the futility of life, he can be found watching cozy mystery shows, daydreaming of his future kaftan collection, or scouring used book vendors to accumulate more vintage romances and mysteries than his shelves are actually capable of handling. One day he plans to travel the world - to see what each country has to offer in the way of used books, movie theatres and dark chocolate, naturally.

moodyboxfan.com
Join the mailing list to keep up-to-date!

Goodreads
https://www.goodreads.com/joshuaian
Facebook
https://www.facebook.com/joshuaianauthor/
Twitter
https://twitter.com/joshuaianauthor
Instagram
https://www.instagram.com/moodyboxfan/
Bookbub
https://www.bookbub.com/authors/joshua-ian

joshuaianauthor@gmail.com

Also By Joshua Ian

Manchester Lake
The Darkly Enchanted Omnibus: A Gothic Romance Collection

Short Stories
All Tall Flowers: A Historical Romance Short
Grave Songs for the Dead: A Short Story Cycle
Gingerbread: A Dark Fiction Short Story
the 1 train: Glimpses of New York City

Keep up-to-date with all of Joshua's current and upcoming projects at moodyboxfan.com

Moody Boxfan Books

Déjà Vu: A Holiday Romance Short by Lawrence I. Hill

Another lonely Christmas for hotel director Alvin. When his high school crush - now R&B superstar Tee Mills - comes to stay, things take a turn. Is this a fated chance to rekindle the first love of his life? Alvin isn't sure he's brave enough to find out. But before the night ends, he'll have his answer - if Tee Mills has anything to say about it.

www.ingramcontent.com/pod-product-compliance
Lightning Source LLC
Chambersburg PA
CBHW031124210626
46816CB00016B/2246